Chap

"Oh what a night!" w

climbed into bed. Kirby and I just went through our wedding rehearsal. What a journey we had taken to get to this day.

I tossed and turned until I was wrapped up in my sheets. My body was trying to shut down but my mind wasn't co-operating.

I looked at the clock beside my bed, for the hundredth time and it was still three o'clock. I could see the stars and moonlight through the sheer panels at my window.

I sat up in bed and stretched. I couldn't help but reminisce about where it all began. I lay back down, pulled the covers up around me, and with great joy relived that first moment until now. I couldn't sleep anyway!

I could lay here for hours barely touching the surface of our years together. In twelve hours, I would marry my neighbor, best friend, and the man I have known and loved for most of my life. Years of hoping, waiting and planning would become a reality today.

We've known each other since the fourth grade. We shared a duplex on a dead end street called Bon-Air St. Kirby and his family lived at 549 and we lived at 547. Neither one of us had a sibling so there was no choice for us but to be friends.

The street ran uphill and there was a concrete ditch that ran through the middle of the street with a bridge on each side.

The homes on Bon-Air were very modest. Around the corner was a church with a big field on the back lot. That's where we played baseball when we could get enough players.

Kirby and I played football and baseball all the time, but he would never play dolls with me. I got it!

If we got snow during the winter time, our street was a great place to go sledding. Neither one of us had a sled so we got boxes from the store on the corner and they worked out just fine until they got really wet!

We figured out a way to communicate without using the phone. One of us would knock on the wall a few times then we would meet outside.

It almost seemed as if we were family. We went to the same school and church. We came to learn a lot about each other. I learned to play the piano and Kirby sang. He had a great voice.

Before we knew it, we were both in high school. When we started the ninth grade our parents let us walk to school. We both decided to join the band. I learned to play the flute and Kirby played the drums.

We were both considered geeks! We made all A's and both had braces on our teeth. I was skinny with red hair, and Kirby was so tall that his pants always looked too short. Worse than that, we both had cases of acne breakouts. In our day we called them, zits!

Being popular was something neither one of us felt was important. Honor roll was and our parents demanded it. We studied together at school and at home. We were anxious to prove ourselves not only to our parents, but the rest of the world.

Summer evenings we sat in the front yard and talked under the watchful eyes of our parents. Both duplexes had a big picture window on the front. We had little time to become anything but friends. I don't think we were really ready for all that mushy stuff! Our parents were always visible.

As we went from childhood to young adults our relationship grew. We went from neighbors, to friends, to classmates then boyfriend and girlfriend. By the time we were sophomores our parents gave us some freedom, and we began to date.

I remember our first kiss! It was a cold night, and we had just played in the half time show at a football game. When we got back to the bleachers, Kirby put his arm around me to help get me warm, and our eyes met.

In that moment we both knew our feelings were more than friendship. I thought to myself, "kiss me!" and he did! After that, there were more kisses than I could count!

I looked at Kirby and asked, "Should we tell our parents or do you think they've figured it out?"

"I think the answer to both of those questions, Ruby, is yes!" He replied with a smile. Little did they know that we rarely held hands!

By the time we were seniors, I knew our relationship was true love. I told him we needed to talk about where we were going as a couple. Spring break was a week away, and we could talk then.

We went to an early show on Saturday and then went and got something to eat. I always wanted to be a teacher maybe even special education. Kirby loved working on cars, but he was fascinated with welding

The nearest college was about two hundred miles away. It offered the courses we both wanted to take. Neither one of our families could afford full tuition. A scholarship was our only option for college.

I took Kirby's hand and said, "We just planned the beginning of our future!"

Graduation day came and our parents were more proud than we imagined! I was Valedictorian and he was Salutatorian. Being number one was always a challenge between us, but I won! We both got full scholarships.

At dinner that night we told our parents that we were in love, but our goal was to finish college, get good jobs and then get married. As usual, both our moms cried and wished us well.

My dad said, "We figured this out a long time ago!"

Kirby's dad laughed and said, "I knew it after the first knock on the wall!"

A month later, Kirby and I were packed and ready to go to college. We assured our parents that our education came first, and we had decided to wait to have sex until we were married.

You could see a sigh of relief on their faces! As we drove off Kirby said, "I bet that blew their minds!" We both just laughed.

Chapter Two

College was a privilege to us and we intended to learn all we could and have the best life possible. We wanted it all and this was the way to get it.

When we got to the campus, our dorms were across the courtyard from each other. How would we really react not being under the watchful eyes of our parents?

We got settled in and took a tour of the campus. Even though it was a small college it was big time to us.

We both decided to find part-time jobs as long as it didn't interfere with our classes. There was a bar about a block from school. I got a job waiting tables and Kirby worked in the kitchen.

Every moment seemed to be filled with something. We had our most fun times when we traveled with the band for the out of town games.

It was a different world here. Life was showing us many things. We were enjoying our freedom, but we missed our families and couldn't wait for the holidays so we could go home.

Four years went by quickly and graduation day was here. We were both graduating in the top of our class. All our hard work had paid off!

The day of the ceremony was beautiful. Our parents were here and they couldn't stop telling us how proud they were of us. It was apparent their hopes and dreams had come true, too!

After the festivities, we all went to dinner then Kirby and I went to celebrate on our own. The steps we had taken on our journey would give us the ability and tools to have a good job and good life.

When we got to the café, Kirby ordered a bottle of wine, poured us a glass and said, "I'll make the first toast."

We raised our glasses, and he said in a loud voice, almost everyone heard him, "I have loved you for twelve years. Will you marry me?"

He stood up, walked around the table and got down on one knee. People in the café begin to clap as I kissed his face and replied, "Yes!"

Tears filled my eyes. I couldn't speak! He took my hand and placed a beautiful diamond ring on it. He kissed me and then whispered softly, "I hid a lot of my tips!"

I began to weep, and people begin to look. Kirby stood up with his glass in his hand and shouted, "She has accepted my proposal of marriage!"

We talked and decided to get married when we could pay for our own wedding. Our parents would always help us, but this we would do on our own.

The next morning, before our parents started home we told them our news! They were overjoyed. We told them that when we got home we would discuss the wedding plans.

By later that afternoon our dorm rooms were empty, and we were headed home. That word really sounded good.

We were going to continue living with our parents until the wedding. Staying in our hometown was important to both of us. Our family, friends and church meant everything.

Two weeks later, Kirby's welding skills paid off, and he got a job. I applied for a teaching job at our old high school and got it.

Now we could plan our wedding. We both wanted to be married at Calvary Church. We had gone there all our lives. It was a beautiful church with special meaning to both of us.

Calvary, just its name gives me goosebumps!

This church has a regal but simple façade. Three sets of white double doors invite you in. The foyer makes you stop and take its beauty in. In the center of the room a large, round wooden table holds a magnificent floral arrangement.

To the left is a beautiful winding staircase that takes you up to the second floor. Most impressive is the sanctuary. When you open one of the doors and walk in, a beautiful stained glass cross is at the top of the highest wall. It causes you to stop and admire its beauty and purpose.

As you walk down the aisle toward the front the piano is on the left and the organ is on the right. Four alters surround that area. There are six steps that take you up to the Baptistery where Brother Paul and the choir are.

For a Christian, being in God's house is a privilege. There's just something about it!

Chapter Three

Then, there's Brother Paul. He came to Calvary Church as a young pastor, but his early dreams in life were to become a golf pro. Maybe open a golf shop, or teach golf.

God had a different plan, and brought him and his family to Calvary at the age of twenty eight. With room to grow and work to do a congregation of one hundred and twenty grew to over three hundred in a few years.

Just when I think I have him figured out, he throws me a curve. His voice is low as he looks across the congregation, and his smile makes me wonder what he's up to!

How does a man of God deal with so many peoples' problems without going crazy? Maybe he is. Just like the rest of us!

Does he know the touch of God's hand? Does he know the sound of His voice? How could he not!

How does one man deal with so much and find time for his own life. I wonder how his family accepts, or tolerates him being a messenger of God. Dumb question on my part. God knows what He's doing!

Brother Paul's humbleness and his love for God define him. He has been given a great task. The teaching of a never ending story of God's love, the Bible. To learn it, to love it, to live it!

He seemed to capture the love of both the young people and the older people. He is a dynamic speaker. I only found one fault with him. It's his choice of his favorite college football team, but he didn't like my choice either!

Though we never discussed our rivalry, sometimes our choice of colors said it all!

Before Brother Paul turned forty, tragedy would strike Calvary. April the twentieth, 2003, Easter Sunday night about ten p.m., lightning struck the church. It smoldered until two a.m.

Disbelief and getting a plan of action happened quickly. Courage and strength, two things that defined Calvary would now be put to the test.

Faith and love in God brought this magnificent church back from ashes. This church has seen joy, death, and destruction. Yet every time I walk through its doors, I thank God it's still standing. Calvary has a very special place in my heart.

There's always a friendly voice inviting you in to a conversation at Calvary. To behold its beauty and purpose is a blessing.

The stars and moonlight were changing to a beautiful sunrise as I closed my eyes and tried to sleep.

A knock on my door startled me as my mom said, "Better get up! We've got a wedding to get ready for!"

I sat up in bed as if I had slept for days. Then I jumped out of bed, did the happy dance and begin to hum the wedding march. "Oh yes, this is my day!" I yelled out.

I got dressed and went to the kitchen. Mom was sitting at the table. As I sat down she wiped her eyes and took my hand. We sat there for a moment and barely able to speak she said, "Oh how I have loved you!"

Emotion took over, and we both wept. There is a tremendous love between my mom and I. Words are not always necessary.

My dad walked in and said with a smile, "Happy day, no more tears! Who's cooking my breakfast?"

Mom and I laughed and she asked, "Why don't you cook breakfast for us this morning?"

He put his hands up in the air and replied, "I never have cooked breakfast, but I will try!" We both laughed out loud as he hugged us both.

Mom fixed a wonderful breakfast. All our favorites, homemade biscuits, fried eggs, coffee and her special tomato gravy!

We all held hands as dad said grace. I squeezed their hands especially tight this morning. I helped mom clean up the kitchen then I took all my things to the living room that were going to the church.

We all got dressed and loaded everything in mom's car and left for the church. Dad said, "You don't need me yet, I'll be there soon." Then he took my hand and whispered, "I can't wait to walk you down the aisle."

I began to cry. He shook his head no, then wiped a tear from my cheek. I kissed his face and replied, "Don't be late!" As we drove away I saw him wipe his eyes with his handkerchief.

Mom smiled and said, "Only happy thoughts today. No more tears." When we pulled up at the church two of mom's friends came out and helped us unload the car.

After we got everything to the bride's room, one of the ladies said, "Come and look at the reception hall." The closer we got to the door the smells made me hungry. She opened the door and said with her arm forward, "You first!"

I took a deep breath and stepped through the door. I couldn't speak and could barely breathe. I never imagined something so beautiful. Every table was sprinkled with rose petals. Set to perfection with china and silverware from the church.

A rose was wrapped around every napkin. There were two buffet tables for the food, three dessert tables and then standing alone on its own table was the wedding cake.

Four tiers of a white cake lined with roses and vines as if it was sitting in my mother's garden. The topper was my mom's. A bride and groom holding hands and facing each other. Her surprise to me!

Mom wrapped her arms around me and said, "Hope you like it, Ruby!" She looked at me barely able to speak. Then took my arm, and I felt her hand trembling as she said, "You are worthy of all that life has to offer."

Brother Paul stuck his head in the door and remarked, "If that's the way you're going down the aisle I'm overdressed!"

I shook my head and thought, "that's one for him!"

Chapter Four

Mom and I went back to the Brides room and Kirby's mom, Fannie, was waiting. She has been like a second mother to me. As I unpacked my bag and laid everything out, I was reminded of how I made these choices.

A year ago before our wedding I began shopping for my dress. When I found it, it was on sale, but I still had to put it in the lay-a-way.

My mom wanted me to wear her pearl necklace and earrings. That was something borrowed.

Fannie gave me Kirby's grandmother's handkerchief and suggested that I have it wrapped around the stems of my bouquet. That was something old.

In a magazine a bride wore ballerina shoes. I thought that was a great idea since Kirby and I were the about the same height. I found a pair of blue ribbons to lace them with. That was something blue.

Mom and Fannie were whispering. "What's going on," I asked?

Fannie pulled a beautifully wrapped box from beside the table and handed it to me. "Don't be angry!" She said softly. "I made this for you."

"I'm going to cry again," I whispered as I covered my face. Unwrapping the gift made me remember that she loved me, too.

I opened the box and folded the tissue paper back. I stood up and screamed with delight! It was a veil. Lace and beads on both sides. I gently pulled it out of the box and it just kept coming!

"It's twelve feet long. I took lace and beads from mine and your mother's wedding dresses to make this for you." Fannie said with tears in her eyes.

I couldn't speak. I hugged her neck as tight as I could and cried again. My mom joined in our hug and then she said, "Enough, enough, it's almost time!"

I was ready to put on my dress, but they were still fussing over my hair and jewelry. My mom unzipped my dress bag, and when she took it out it took my breath away.

I stepped into it and mom buttoned up the back. Then Fannie put the veil on me. Without warning they both started taking pictures.

All of a sudden, there was a knock on the door. It was my dad. He said, "Both mothers to the chapel to be seated, and my daughter on my arm." They both stood beside me, and I told him to come in. When he opened the door, the look on his face said it all!

I kissed both moms, thanked them and said with a smile, "see you in a minute." I picked up my bouquet. Took my dad's arm, and we walked toward the double doors going into the sanctuary.

My Maid of Honor was my best friend, Sharon, and Kirby's Best Man was his father. The music began, and Sharon started her walk. When she was in place, my dad and I stepped in the doorway.

The smell of roses was sweet and welcoming. They were everywhere. Red roses were attached to ribbons at the end of every pew. The arbor was covered in red, yellow and white roses.

Eight candelabras were wrapped from top to bottom in white roses. Six beautiful fern baskets with trailing babies' breath lined both sides of the steps going up to the arbor.

There was no doubt in my mind that Ms. Ava Sue helped put all this together. She's the best! Her flower shop is the oldest one in town, and her work is in demand by everyone!

Her kindness and beautiful smile are always visible and welcoming. Her arrangements are as magnificent as ones you find in a magazine.

The wedding march began and everyone stood up. I kissed my dad's hand, and we started down the aisle. The lights in the sanctuary were down low and the soft light from the candelabras guided us.

Kirby was standing at the arbor with Brother Paul. He was such a handsome man. My man. My heart was racing so fast that I opened my mouth to breathe.

My father kissed my face and gave my hand to Kirby. Brother Paul said, "Let's take a look back before we begin." Kirby and I looked at each other wondering where this was coming from!

Brother Paul said, "I've watched two children grow to adults. A faith that has grown in their walk with God has built a relationship that has beat all odds, and that is why we are here today!"

"I could tell you many more stories about these two." He said with a smile. Then he looked at both of us and remarked, "Not today." At that moment, I really needed to go to the bathroom!

Brother Paul began again and when it was time for us to say our vows it really got strange. He looked at Kirby and said, "Repeat after me! I promise to love, honor, cherish, obey, give shopping privileges, never complain about a cooked meal and try to remember you're always right, until death do us part!"

Kirby looked at Brother Paul as if to say, "What is this!" Brother Paul put his hands up in the air as if to say, "Do you?"

Finally, Kirby said, "I do."

Then he looked at me with a strange smile and said, "Repeat after me! I promise to love, honor, cherish, obey, know that you are the head of our family, clean the house and take care of the children, until death us do part!"

I looked at Brother Paul, laughed out loud and replied, "With God's help, I do!"

We exchanged rings then Brother Paul addressed the guests and said, "Now that's a commitment! I pronounce you husband and wife. You may kiss your bride!"

Kirby lifted my veil, put one hand on each side of my face, and kissed me softly and lovingly.

Brother Paul shouted, "Now that's what I'm talking about. Welcome Kirby and Ruby who are now one in God's, eyes." Everyone stood and clapped as we left the sanctuary.

Kirby and I ran quickly to the ladies' bathroom. He hesitated, but I pulled him in there with me. I couldn't wait any longer and it would be a great story to tell our children.

When we got to the reception hall the party had already started. Music was playing. Our guest were eating and dancing. We visited with all of our guests then we were seated at our special table.

Before long, it was time to cut the cake. I reminded Kirby not to smash that cake on my face because I would retaliate! He laughed so hard that when he did respond his words were, "Food fight might be interesting! It's already been a crazy day!"

With his hand on mine, I cut a small piece of cake to lessen the damage if it happened! I gently put a small bite in his mouth and whispered, "Be kind!"

He got a small bite, held it up to my lips and smiled. Then he gently put it in my mouth. Both our parents made a toast to us and wished us the very best.

It was time for us to say our good-byes and thank everyone for coming. Kirby and I asked for everyone's attention, and then he spoke.

"Thank you, for making this day the most beautiful one of our lives. We will forever be grateful and thankful for your love and support! We're out of here!"

When we got back to the bride's room, I ran to the bathroom again, we changed clothes and walked to the front door. The center doors were open and everybody was lining the stairs going down to the parking lot.

As we walked down the steps they covered us with rose petals and bird seed. We stopped at the last step and I said, "Get ready ladies, here comes the bouquet!"

I turned and threw it high over my shoulder. Someone let out a scream, and when I looked to see who caught it, I was shocked! It was Ms. Lilly Bell. She was ninety years old and had never been married.

I gave her a thumbs up and said, "You're next baby!"

We had rented a cabin about two hours away in the mountains. Our parents had loaded our car with food, drinks and a nice bottle of wine. All we needed now was our privacy.

I think we were both nervous about our first night as husband and wife. We decided to go slow and time would show us what we needed.

It was dark when we got there. We unloaded the car, fixed us something to eat then opened our bottle of wine. Kirby took my hand, and we sat in the swing on the porch and enjoyed our wine.

We watched the fire flies as they lit up the sky. At the other end of the porch was a hot tub. I decided to make the first move. I kissed Kirby on the side of his face and said, "Let's finish our wine in the hot tub!"

He smiled and replied, "I'll get it ready, go put on your swimsuit."

When I came back out on the porch, he was in the hot tub and the bottle of wine was sitting on the table beside it.

I asked, "Is the water warm?"

"Just like tub water," He responded.

I thought to myself, "Blow his mind and make it a night he will always remember!"

I sat my glass down on the table and started to step in the hot tub. Then I stopped and took off my bathing suit. He turned his wine glass up and drank it all!

He began to laugh and said, "Great idea!" Then he held up his swimming trunks and whispered, "Beat you to it. Now get in here!"

There was no shyness or embarrassment between us. Needless to say, exploring and satisfying took over and that made the wait worthwhile.

As we touched one another the gentle kisses and the racing of our hearts left little doubt of the joy that was ahead.

I had dreamt of this moment a million times, but never imagined the pleasure that God put in placc for a husband and wife.

Chapter Five

It was time to go back home. We packed and loaded the car and would always remember where this moment in our lives began. We sat close to each other on the drive home as if we were on our first date. Love is grand!

A few months before the wedding, we found a one bedroom house for rent that was close to both our parents. They were giving us enough furniture to fill every room.

We both had nice cars so all our extra money would be saved to buy a house. We wanted to be debt free when the time came to start a family. Making that goal a reality would be the challenge.

The first year of our marriage seemed to fly by. We both got good steady jobs. Kirby was working as a welder, and I was teaching. We set a budget and stuck to it!

A golden opportunity came up for me. I was offered the chance to work with children who had disabilities. The school system would pay for my classes, and I could still teach during the day.

Kirby and I talked about it. Even though it would consume a lot of our time together, it was a dream come true for me. Before we knew it, our one year anniversary was in a week.

We were so proud of our accomplishment. In two months I would graduate from my Special Education Class.

It was the beginning of summer, and I was glad to have a break from this past year of all my classes. It had been the most rewarding and challenging year of my life.

Kirby and I decided to start looking for a house. We had worked hard and saved every penny we didn't have to spend.

Mom, Fannie and I rode around town every day looking to see what was out there. We looked at many houses, but they were out of our budget.

We got into some road construction one day and got turned around. As we tried to get back to the main road a *for sale* sign caught our eyes. You couldn't see the house from the road, it sat back behind some huge, old oak trees.

I said, "Hey, let's drive up there and take a look!"

There was fencing all along the front and double gates at the driveway. As we drove up the tree lined driveway, we could see the house within a few seconds.

It was an old farm house. Painted white with green shutters and a tin roof. It had a porch all the way across the front. Most welcoming were the rocking chairs.

Mom said, "Let's get out and take a look!"

"Let me knock on the door and make sure it's alright," I responded.

Fannie yelled out, "Watch for a dog!"

I knocked on the door, but no one answered. We didn't hear a dog bark or see one so we decided to walk and look around.

The grounds were beautiful and well maintained. There was a rope swing in the big oak tree beside the house. We walked around back and there was a patio with a fire pit. Quiet and private, it felt like the perfect place.

We started walking back to the car, and a car was coming up the drive. A woman got out and introduced herself as Nancy, the real estate agent.

We talked for a few minutes and she asked if we wanted to see the inside. We all said, "Yes." She told us that the lady who owned the house had passed away in the nursing home and her daughter was selling it.

We went inside and it was a neat place. The living room had a fireplace, there was a big kitchen with an eating area, two bedrooms and one bathroom. The floors were all wood. There was a stained glass window on each side of the front door with angels in it.

It also had five acres with an orchard. I was looking out the kitchen window and saw an old barn. The agent took us out there and remarked, "These old cyprus boards came from the old lady's home place. Her father's tractor shed was blown down during a storm. She and her husband came and salvaged the lumber and built the barn."

"I love this place," I told her. "What is the asking price?"

"Seventy thousand dollars." She replied.

"We have enough money to pay cash for this place, but it would take all our savings," I thought to myself. Out loud, I said, "May I bring my husband back to look at it?"

The agent replied, "I'll be back here on Saturday about this same time if he would like to see it."

On the drive home Mom and Fannie remarked that they both thought this would be a great place for us. They offered to help us fix it up and make it our home.

I hoped Kirby would love the place, too. I had an advantage! A few days to make him realize how much I wanted this place.

We talked about the house over supper. Depleting our savings was a concern for him, but we had saved for this reason.

Then he said with a smile, "Let's wait and see what Saturday brings!"

I was the most loving, giving wife for the next few days hoping he would realize how much I wanted this place. Although I knew that depleting our savings could put us in a bad situation if something came up and we had no money.

We went back to the house, and I decided to change my strategy. I would tell him that I loved this house at least a hundred times and watch his reaction. We were there about two hours then we went and met our parents for dinner.

Kirby told us all that he loved the house and the land, but didn't want to use all of our savings. Maybe we could make an offer and work something out. I knew he was right. It was up to me to keep my heart from guiding my brain.

Two days later, we made an offer of sixty thousand dollars. This would leave us ten thousand dollars in savings and the ability to replenish our account since we wouldn't have a house note.

Later that evening, Nancy, the agent called us back and said, "Your offer has been accepted. When would you like to close?"

We were overjoyed and now the work began to make it our own. Four days later we closed and were given the keys to our new home. With all the things our family had given us, and a few good yard sales, we could call ourselves home!

Chapter Six

Within a month, our house was fixed up. Kirby and his dad were working on the barn. My dad was on his tractor cutting grass and brush.

In two weeks my summer break would be over and school would begin. I was hoping that there would be a chance for me to use my special education knowledge.

Before long, summer began to welcome fall. The leaves were changing colors, and as they fell to the ground they formed a blanket of colors.

I sometimes dreaded this time of year because a lot of the children came to school sick, and I always seemed to get it next.

Winter was just about over when I caught something. I felt it was a virus because I was nauseous. After fighting it for three days I went to the doctor. His office was full of sick people and this could only make it worse!

The nurse called my name, did my blood work, then she took me to a room. When the doctor came in I told him that I hadn't ever been this sick.

He laughed and said, "It's just part of the process. It won't last long." He listened to my heart, asked me a few questions then smiled and said, "Congratulations!"

I grabbed his arm, looked him in the eyes and asked, "What did you say?"

He hugged me and whispered, "You're pregnant! Blame your husband, not your students!"

Barely able to speak a word I replied, "Morning sickness!" He gave me something for it and told me I was going to be fine. When he left the room, I did the happy dance! A baby, I must have said those words a million times.

I could hardly wait to tell Kirby. This would be the second most memorable night of our lives. He stopped on his way home from work to pick up supper since I had been sick.

I met him at the door and said, "Great! I'm starving!"

We sat down to eat and I told him that I would say, grace. "Oh Lord, God, we thank you for everything, and I do mean everything. Watch over us and keep us safe during this journey. Amen."

While we were eating dinner, I told Kirby that I had some projects that needed to be done. He replied, "I'll add them to my list!" I told him not to take long because we would need them before long.

"What did the doctor say?" he asked. "Probably a virus. It will run its course in a few days."

I said with a smile, "Not exactly, this one will take about nine months!"

He looked at me as he tilted his head to one side. Then he stood up, sat back down and tears filled his eyes. He bowed his head and whispered, "Thank you, God!" Then he stood up and yelled, "We're going to have a baby!"

He picked me up in his arms and twirled me around as if we were dancing. I thought he had lost his mind, but then I realized that he was falling in love with our miracle.

"Does our family know?" He asked.

I responded with a smile, "Not before you!"

He sat me down in my chair and wept like a child. I kissed his face and said, "I love you." Then he carried me to the bedroom and we lay in one another's arms until we fell asleep.

The next morning he woke me with a kiss and I quickly got up and ran to the bathroom. He yelled, "I want to tell everybody!" With my head in the toilet I couldn't help but smile. I never imagined that he would be so overjoyed!

As I stood up from the toilet he came in the bathroom and said, "You go back to bed and rest. I'm going to work and it's going to be a great day!"

I called the school and told them I would be out for a few days. There was no way I could teach from the bathroom!

I started taking the medicine and two days later my morning sickness was better and I went back to school. A week later, it was almost gone. I told everyone that I was pregnant and got enough advice to write a book. I couldn't help but laugh at some of the things they told me to do!

Sunday after church we invited our parents over for lunch and told them about the baby. They were so excited!

When I was seven months pregnant, both our parents got together and planned a baby shower. Needless to say, they sent out so many invitations that it had to be held at the church.

I was excited and a little bit embarrassed. I didn't want people to feel obligated to come and bring a gift. I just wanted them to share in our joy!

Three days prior to the baby shower both our moms started baking. You couldn't imagine all the cookies, cupcakes, pies and cakes in their kitchens.

My Maid of Honor, Sharon, made the punch and provided the ice cream. I reminded her not to spike the punch!

It was a chore for me just to get dressed. My back hurt, and I couldn't reach my feet to put my shoes on.

When I got to the church, the room was beautiful! There were ribbons tied to each chair and balloons tied to every table. The tables were covered with every sweet thing you could think of.

Tears filled my eyes when I saw the gift tables. There must have been fifty gifts so beautifully wrapped. How blessed I felt to be loved by so many.

By two o'clock, every chair at every table was full. It turned out to be a lot of fun. We played games, ate and fellowshipped.

Sharon and I moved to the gift table. She took all the gift tags off the gifts, wrote who each was from, and then handed the gift to me to open.

There were two gifts from Fannie, one for me and one for the baby. I opened the one for me. It was a beautiful story/journal for me called, "Whispers." It had been signed by the author.

It was a book for me to journal my journey through pregnancy. The mother and baby spoke to one another through their whispers. It's one of the few books where the unborn child has a voice. In my opinion, this journal is as important to the mother as a baby book is to the child.

By four thirty I was unwrapping the last gift. Sharon told me there were fifty names on her list. Barely able to speak, I stood and said, "I have never in my life been so touched and honored by your kindness. Thank you, for coming and all you've done."

When people began leaving, Mom and Fannie began taking all the gifts to their cars. We cleaned up the room, packed up all the food and went back to our house.

Kirby was working overtime, or so I thought. While we were at the shower Kirby and both our dads were putting the baby's room together. All the furniture that we looked at and talked about was there. A surprise for me!

I was overwhelmed and broke into tears. Kirby put his arms around me and just held me. "Relax now baby. It's all done, and we're waiting on you."

When our parents left, I decided to take a long, hot bubble bath. I really just wanted to be by myself and have a good cry. Hormones I guess!

When we got home from church, the next day, I started washing all the baby clothes and putting them away. We got so much at the shower that we had very little to buy.

We didn't want to know the sex of our baby before it was born. This gave our moms something to argue about constantly. We didn't care if it was a boy or girl. They didn't either really. One of them was going to be wrong and the other would have bragging rights!

Chapter Seven

It was about two in the morning when I thought I was having contractions. I wasn't sure, but before long I woke Kirby up and told him it was time. He got dressed and took me and my bag to the car.

When we got to the hospital, they took us to a room. The doctor came in and said, "You're in labor and it could be anytime between now and twenty four hours."

I looked at him and replied in a high pitched tone, "I won't be sane if this goes on for twenty four hours!"

Kirby took my hand and whispered, "I'm going to call our parents. It might be a long wait, but they don't want to miss this!"

They hooked me up to everything needed to monitor the baby while Kirby made the calls. My pain was getting more intense! There was a nurse in my room at all times.

The pain was very intense and my attitude was right there with it! Kirby was holding my hand, saying, "Breathe!" I gave him a look and about that time the doctor came in, checked me out and said, "It's time to push!"

I was pushing and praying at the same time. All of a sudden, my body relaxed, and I heard a faint cry. The doctor held the baby up and said, "Here he is, he looks good to me!"

Kirby let out a scream, "I have a son, a baby boy, my son!"

I tried to breathe, but all I could do was weep. They cleaned him up, wrapped him in a blanket and put him in my arms. I kissed his nose then put him in Kirby's arms. He whispered as he kissed his face, "Welcome to your family. I've waited on you for a long time."

Our parents came in and were overjoyed! The doctor put him in the incubator and our parents stood around it and cherished every moment!

The doctor said, "Let's get him upstairs and check him out, and he'll be back in a little while." Kirby lay down on the bed beside me and wept. Our parents stayed a few minutes then they left to go get breakfast.

My mom leaned over, kissed me and said, "You did a great job! We'll be back this afternoon." As they were leaving a woman came in with two breakfast trays. We held hands and Kirby said grace.

"Oh Lord, you have given us a miracle, and we thank you. May you always know that we love you."

After we ate, we both fell asleep. About ten thirty, the doctor came in and said, "He weighs seven pounds and is twenty one inches long. His health is good! We found a film on both his eyes, so I have called in a specialist to check them out."

Kirby stood up and there was another knock on the door. The nurse had brought the baby for his feeding. Kirby walked over to the bassinet, picked him up and brought him to me.

We both looked into his eyes but could see nothing. "Feed that boy, Momma!" he said. "He needs a name, too!" We decided if it was a boy we would name him Bud.

The doctor left, and I nursed my baby as we watched him and told him how very much he was loved. About thirty minutes later, the nurse came back to the room and got him so they could check his eyes.

"Probably nothing," Kirby said. "Whatever it is they will fix it."

There was another knock on the door. In came two girls with flowers and balloons. No doubt from our parents.

Kirby handed me my robe and said, "Let's take a walk if you feel like it!"

"Great idea!" I responded. It felt good to get up and walk. I needed to build my strength before we took Bud home.

When we got back to the room, we were both quiet. Hoping and praying that everything would check out fine with Bud's eyes.

Brother Paul came to congratulate us and check on everyone. While he was there the doctor came back.

The doctor said, "We've done some tests, taken some tissue, and we've found something!"

Brother Paul stood up and stepped toward my side of the bed. Kirby was on the other side, and we all held hands.

"There's no easy way to say this. Bud's blind, but we believe that he can hear and will be able to talk because he cries."

I covered my mouth with my hands to muffle my scream. Kirby covered his face with his hands and wept.

Brother Paul asked, "Can surgery correct this?"

The doctor replied, "For now, no, but they are doing research all the time. More tests will tell us if a transplant would be possible. We are letting you and Bud go home tomorrow. I am sending books and all information about blindness home with you."

He left the room and Brother Paul said, "God gives special gifts to special people. Bud can have a good life. Blind people live on their own and function every day."

Brother Paul left, and Mom called to check on us. I told her we were going home tomorrow. She said, "We'll see you then. Fannie and I have cooked up enough food so you won't have to do anything but take care of Bud."

I didn't tell her that Bud was blind. We were trying to find a way to accept it ourselves. The door opened and the nurse rolled the bassinet in. She put Bud in my arms and said, "I'll be back later."

I stared deeply into his beautiful blue eyes and whispered, "We will love you, protect you, teach you, but never stop praying for the miracle of your sight."

Kirby took him in his arms, looked at me and remarked, "If he's perfect in every way, but for his sight, we've already got a miracle!"

At that moment, I realized that he was right. I am a teacher. I can learn about blindness and teach us all. Maybe even help someone else along the way.

"You're absolutely right!" Kirby said. "I'll work two jobs if necessary. He will have everything he needs!"

Chapter Eight

The next morning, they brought Bud to our room with a stack of books on blindness. "He'll never leave my sight again!" I told Kirby. "I'll be his eyes and his guide as long as he needs me to be."

Cars lined the street as we pulled up the drive. Family, friends and neighbors all waiting to meet Bud and offer their support and help.

Brother Paul was standing on the porch, and I couldn't help but smile as I whispered, "Thank you, God." Brother Paul took Bud in his arms and said, "Let's pray."

God's people were standing in our front yard praying for our family. All the problems didn't seem relevant at this moment.

When Brother Paul finished everyone wished us well and offered their help if needed. I looked at everyone and said, "Thank you would never be enough for all you've done."

When we got inside the house, I cried like a baby. There was food everywhere and more gifts for Bud. On the refrigerator door was a list of names and phone numbers in the event we needed help.

I laid Bud in his crib, then Kirby and I just held each other. He kissed me on my cheek and whispered, "How blessed we are that God chose us for this very special blessing. Not everyone can do what we are going to do."

"How right you are!" I replied. "It's pretty cool being high up on God's list."

He just shook his head and remarked, "God gave you two challenges!"

We both laughed. Something we hadn't done in a few days.

When we got to the table our parents were waiting. My father said grace, and I started to cry. "What's wrong?" he asked.

Kirby took my hand and with tears in his eyes, said, "Bud's blind." That was a life changing moment for all of us.

You could tell they were in shock. No one said a word. We told them all we knew, and then Kirby's dad stood up and said, "He'll have four more sets of eyes to teach and guide him. You won't have to do it alone."

After dinner and cleaning up the kitchen, our parents left. We went to Bud's room to check on him, and I whispered, "Mommy and Daddy love you!" He turned his head toward us! A sign that he could hear.

I took him to our room and fed him. Then we laid him between us. Kirby fell off to sleep quickly, so I turned on my bedside light and begin looking through some of the books about blindness.

I was blown away about so many programs for the blind. There was a brochure about classes for people interested in working with the blind. There were only a few places in the state that offered these classes. They were expensive, and I needed to find out if a grant was available.

I finally put the books aside and turned out the light. I kissed Bud's head and whispered, "It's going to be fine."

No sooner than I fell off to sleep, Bud began to cry. Kirby raised up and said, as he laughed, "Two a.m. feeding, Mom!" After I nursed him, I held him in my arms, and we both went back to sleep.

The smell of coffee brewing woke me up. Bud was still asleep so I laid him on Kirby's side and went to the kitchen. We sat at the table and talked about what we needed to do.

Kirby was going back to work, and I was going to resign from school. I wanted and needed to be home with Bud. I knew I could depend on our moms if I had to go somewhere, but not daily. That was my job!

I told Kirby that I wanted to take some classes on working with the blind. He felt it was a good idea, and then I could teach him, and we could multi task.

He went to the shower because we were going to church in a few hours. I decided not to take Bud to the nursery. I was being over protective. Something I would probably do for the rest of my life.

Brother Paul was waiting in the foyer when we walked through the doors. He said, "Good morning, I would love to welcome Bud to Calvary this morning. What can I tell the congregation?"

"We want everyone to know about Bud's blindness. It's easier for you to tell them all at one time than for us to try to tell them one on one." Kirby replied.

When Brother Paul stepped up to the podium, I took a deep breath and held Kirby's hand. We walked down the aisle and stood beside him. He took Bud in his arms and said, "It's an honor and privilege to welcome our newest member, Bud, to Calvary's family."

Everyone clapped and then Brother Paul asked everyone to stand, hold hands and pray.

"We thank you, Lord God, for this miracle of life. May he always feel your love and know you're close. Protect him and let not his blindness hinder one moment of his life."

You could hear the gasps as Brother Paul told everyone they could be seated. We walked back to our seats and Brother Paul proceeded to preach his sermon. When church was dismissed, almost everyone came over to us and offered their love and support.

Brother Paul is a pretty smart man. He mentioned Bud's blindness, but didn't dwell on it. He gave it to God, in prayer.

As we walked out of church, I realized that if Bud could walk, talk and hear, this handicap would just be a stepping stone in his life.

Later that evening the phone calls started pouring in. Friends and church members offering their help. I thought to myself, "This is what God's people do, and they haven't failed us!"

Chapter Nine

The next morning, Kirby went to work. Before long, Mom and Fannie came by to see if I needed anything. I asked them to sit with Bud while I went to school and resigned. We would miss the money, but for now I needed to be home with Bud.

When I got back home, Fannie was on the couch holding Bud, and my mom was right beside her. I looked at them and asked, "Has he been held the whole time I've been gone?"

They both nodded their heads, yes! I threw my hands up in the air, laughed and said, "That's ok, I intend on spoiling him, too!"

We were all sitting down when my mom and Fannie began to convince me that I was unprepared to raise a blind child. I immediately took offense!

My mom said, "If you can, find a class to teach you how to help Bud. Let us watch him, and you go learn all you can." I cried as I stood up and walked out of the room.

Fannie came to me, put her arms around me and remarked, "He's not affected by his blindness now, as much as he will be in a year. Go to school now! Then you can teach all of us."

I knew they were right, and I felt so blessed to have them. Over the next few days I read all the books, and called about finding a class. There was a class available and it cost three hundred dollars. If you were a teacher it was free, but it was four days long and a hundred miles away.

I discussed it with our moms, and they agreed to stay with Bud and Kirby until I got back. Kirby and I discussed the classes over dinner and he said, "I'll work all the overtime available. Whatever Bud needs we will do our best to give to him."

Two days later, I was on my way to school. I was excited and scared at the same time. When I pulled up to the school, I wasn't expecting what I saw. People were sitting around outside, walking around and talking. I underestimated what life could be like for someone blind.

I went inside and the Director was waiting for me. She introduced herself as Ms. Eleanor. We shook hands and she said, "Prepare to learn to live in a blind person's world before you can put him in yours."

She took me to a room where three other ladies were waiting. They were here because they had blind children, too. She looked at us and said, "You will be the caregiver and teacher to your children. We will teach you the skills to give them the richest life possible."

I was praying this program would give me hope and confidence. We got our luggage, and then she took us to our rooms. A few minutes later, we went to the cafeteria for lunch. An hour later our classes would begin.

While we were sitting at our table, I watched in awe at how these students functioned! All the condiments on the table had rubber bands on them. I thought to myself,

"This is the neatest thing I've ever seen. One for mayo, two for mustard and three for ketchup!"

When we got in class, I was overwhelmed at what we needed to learn, not only to teach, but to help protect them.

The first thing she taught us was to not let them become dependent on us. They need to perform tasks for themselves. What you teach is as important as how you teach it. When progress is slow, do not get frustrated or aggravated.

A schedule is very important. You must keep them on it. It helps define the day from night by activities and meals. Sound is as important. It allows the child to identify who is talking and where you are.

Most important, when you feel sad, go to another room to deal with it. You must stay connected.

When you are outside carry a beeper where the child can find you. Pay attention to their eyes since they have no blink reflex and remember that windy conditions reduce their ability to hear clearly.

By the end of the first day I was worn out. I had so much to remember and learn to use that I couldn't imagine not being here. The next two days were just as hard. We began learning Brail! This really blew my mind!

The last day was our biggest challenge! I was ready to go to the dining room for breakfast when someone knocked on my door.

I opened it and a young girl said, "I'm here to be your guide today." Then she handed me a blindfold and a cane.

"Surely not!" I thought.

"You will learn to function in our world today!" she said. I put the blindfold on, took her arm and closed the door. She told me there were one hundred and twenty steps to the dining room. For some reason I kept walking to the right. Eventually, I ran into the wall and lost my count.

I stopped and said, "Wait a minute. This is crazy!"

She replied, "Welcome to a blind person's world, and our day is just getting started!"

I used the cane to keep me from running into the wall again, but I hit several people swinging it from side to side. She got me to our table, and when I sat down I just barely caught the edge of my chair. I yelled out and everyone else laughed!

She told me that our drinks were put on the table by the staff, but we fix our own plates from the buffet. Every dish is listed in brail above it.

Not only could I not read Brail, but how was I going to find our table, and worse than that get to the table with everything still on my plate!

She laughed and said, "Stay with me and I'll help you."

Was I in over my head? I was in a new world and needed help. I never realized what it was like for someone who was blind. Boy, did I have a lot to learn!

When this day was over, and I got back to my room, I sat on the foot of the bed and cried. I was scared and sore. I fell at least three times and poked I don't know how many students with my cane. It would have been much worse without my guide!

I called home to check on everyone. Kirby said, "Bud is so spoiled it's not funny. He's been held since you've been gone." Then he asked me about my day!

I managed a laugh and replied, "It's been awful! I had to wear a blindfold as if I were blind. Learning to function as they do is really hard. I can't wait to put that blindfold on you so you will know what I've been through. I'll be home tomorrow. See you then."

Chapter Ten

Over the next two months we watched Bud change and grow. He was kicking his legs, moving his arms and beginning to coo and smile. We took comfort knowing that he could hear and hopefully talk.

By the time Bud was six months old, I could read brail and had read at least twenty books on working with the blind. My mom and Fannie were a constant source of help with Bud.

As Bud began to roll over and pull himself up, I told Kirby that we needed to move everything that could cause him harm. Especially, anything that he could fall on, or put in his mouth!

I put him in his walker and guided him with my voice. I learned that it was important to let him know where I was. I never had a problem keeping his attention. He was always eager to learn.

He had many toys. Mostly stuffed and musical. We sat in the floor, and I taught him about playing ball. That was difficult! Daily I would take his hand, have him touch things and tell him what they were.

I never realized how important words were until I repeated them daily. Between the children's programs on television and the radio Bud began to learn and sing songs.

I was told to keep him on a very tight schedule since he couldn't tell the difference between night and day. Especially, not to let him become dependent on me. He needed to perform tasks and interact.

He needed a safe spot. This was Kirby's chair. I told everyone that came to the house to always speak when they enter the room. I wanted him to be able to identify their voice.

At nine months, he began to stand up and try to walk. He was already crawling. We put up a baby gate, moved all the furniture out of the room except the couch and chair. This room became his space.

As Bud began to grow and learn, life got very interesting. He had the ability to remember things after being told only a few times.

By the time Bud was one year old, there were very few things he couldn't do. He never slowed down! Kirby always commented about the way Bud touched everything. I told him that Bud did that because his hands were his eyes.

I would put his hand on Kirby's face and hair then say, "Daddy." Then I would let him touch my face and hair, and then say, "Mommy."

Kirby picked him up one night and said, "Bedtime Bud, let's go get your pajamas on." Bud touched his face, then his hair and said, "Daddy!"

Kirby looked at me and laughed out loud then remarked, "I was first! He said Daddy first!"

I thought to myself, "You little traitor!" Then I looked up with a smile on my face and whispered, "Thank you, God, that he can hear and speak!"

Kirby held Bud close, and they did the happy dance all the way to his room. I agonized over Bud's blindness, but I failed to realize that this was the only life he knew.

When Bud was three years old we got a special Christmas Eve present. It began to snow. After several hours there was enough snow on the ground to build a snowman.

We put on our coats, hats and boots, bundled Bud up and couldn't wait to watch his reaction to the snow. Kirby started rolling the body, for a snowman, and I put Bud down in the snow and let him touch it! I told him to stick his tongue out and the snowflakes would fall on it!

He was having a blast! He rolled in it, threw it up in the air, and then we made him a snowball. His smile and laughter said it all. I realized that our life was not that difficult, just different!

When Kirby finished the snowman, Bud touched it all over and said, "Three balls Dad, and a hat!" We just stood there amazed at the things he knew. Our hard work was paying off.

"What a great Christmas." Kirby said as he picked Bud up and held him in his arms. We were all freezing, but by the time we convinced Bud to go inside it was almost dark.

After supper and a hot bath we finally convinced Bud that Santa only came when everyone was asleep.

Christmas morning Bud woke up yelling, "Santa!"

Kirby went and got him while I put on a pot of coffee. We sat down in the living room floor, and let Bud open his presents. I explained them one by one so that he would know what they were.

"One more," Kirby said as he walked Bud over to his wagon. Bud touched every inch of it. He turned the wheels then Kirby told him to climb in. I put one hand on each side and said, "Hold on!" Then I began to pull it around the room.

Kirby began picking up all the wrapping paper when our parents showed up with more presents and work. After our parents made two trips to their cars to get presents I remarked, "Went a little overboard, don't you think!"

They just smiled and shook their heads. Kirby and I looked at each other and all we could say was thank you. I prepared a big breakfast, and when we sat down to eat, Kirby's father said grace.

"Oh God, you have richly blessed us. Happy Birthday to Jesus, your son. The real reason for Christmas day! Amen."

Bud quickly turned his head and said, "Jesus, let's sing Jesus!"

"Ok!" I replied. Then Bud led us all the way through the song, "Jesus loves me." What a great way to start Christmas morning.

After our parents left, I cleaned up the kitchen while Kirby played with Bud and his new toys. It got quiet, and I got concerned so I looked through the doorway into the living room.

Kirby was asleep on the floor, and Bud was asleep in the wagon. I got my camera and preserved that moment for all time!

Bud sat in his wagon every day. When spring came, I would pull him, and tell him about everything I saw. He especially loved riding by Mr. John's farm because he got to touch the goats and dogs. Then we rode by Ms. Patricia's house so he could smell her baking. Sometimes, she would leave him a sack.

Kirby had welded a top over the wagon to help block the sun. My mom made a cushion so his ride would be more comfortable. I taught him to recognize the difference between the grass and the road. I think he loved the road best because of the bumps!

Before we knew it, Bud was six years old. He could do a lot for himself, but I always kept a watchful eye.

Bud loved Sunday school and being around other children, especially Anna. Everyone treated Bud with compassion except the two brothers, Jack and Jim. They were mean as snakes! Jack had a strange laugh that sounded like a snorting pig. They called Bud names and laughed at him, but Anna always came to his rescue!

Anna had a special place in her heart for Bud. Maybe it was because her father was deaf. There was another boy, Joey, that was crippled. Jack and Jim called him "Duck" because of the way he walked. They said,

"Watch him waddle!" They said cruel things about her father, too, but always denied it!

While Bud was in children's church, I visited with friends. I always went down to pew number four and sat with Ms. Faye. She was a widow woman with a beautiful smile and attitude. We talked about how our week was but mostly about our costume jewelry. We laughed about how real they looked.

When I went back to where I usually sat, I was always welcomed by Ms. Mary and her husband, Mr. Joe. She always hugged my neck and said, "Good morning." What a great way to start the day!

When I was in town and drove by their house, most times Mr. Joe would be outside on his riding mower cutting the grass. They have a beautiful home, but one thing always caught my eye! Colonel Reb on the front porch! They were Ole Miss fans, too!

Usually before the service started, Ms. Patricia would come from Sunday school and sit beside me. She was the town's best baker! She made wonderful desserts and her food was good, too!

She always asked, "Can I sit with you this morning?" I always told her, sure. I really enjoyed her company. A while back, her mother came to Calvary. We would sit and talk while she waited on Ms. Patricia.

As she got older, she didn't come anymore, but I sure enjoyed talking with her because she reminded me of my mother. I couldn't imagine missing church at Calvary and not sharing this day with such wonderful friends. The icing on my cake was sharing my time with God, in his house.

Before long, Bud turned eight years old and told me he wanted to play the piano at church. He already sang in the choir. I talked to Mr. Chuck and he said, "Once he learns to read brail, we'll get some brail piano key covers and we'll work on it." That time was now because I was ready to teach it to him. I felt that I had learned it well enough.

Before long, Anna and Bud were almost inseparable. She was at our house almost every day after school. She was very protective of Bud. They would sit on the porch and talk and laugh. She probably was as protective of her father.

When Bud turned twelve, Kirby bought a set of walkie-talkies. He told Bud that it was a special way for them to talk. They came with cases, so Kirby put one on his belt and one on Bud's. He taught him how to use it and told him to always keep it in the case. They would come in handy if one of them got lost or hurt.

Christmas was just around the corner. Bud had mastered brail, so his grandparents went together and got him an old piano. Kirby and I ordered the brail key pad covers, and Mr. Chuck was ready to teach him to play.

There was nothing he wouldn't try, and there was always someone willing to help him. By the age of fifteen, he was playing the piano and singing at church. I would have never imagined all that he could accomplish, but with God's help all things are possible.

Bud seemed content with his life. We always wondered if there was anything we could do different. He knew nothing of our world, and had mastered everything in his. He was always happy and we made sure he always felt loved. If ever he wanted to try something new, we made sure he got that opportunity.

Life with Bud was more exciting than challenging. He never met a stranger, and knew most people by their voice. It was amazing how he managed to do so many things. We were the only ones that knew he had a disability. He didn't!

Chapter Eleven

Today was the church bazaar. Kirby had to work so I was taking Bud and Anna. We would go early to carry all the baked goods, and set up our table.

Kirby helped load the car, and then he started down the driveway to work. As he drove off, he yelled out," I'll meet you at the church when I can."

By lunchtime, the church grounds were covered with people eating, singing, and playing games. Bud was with Anna, and they were having a great time.

Our parents had the booth next to ours, and they had sold almost everything they baked. I walked around and talked to some of our friends. One lady told that her husband, a fireman, was just called to work. We all knew there must be a fire somewhere.

About two o'clock, the radio was breaking news about an explosion at the gas plant. My heart stopped, and I fell to the ground. My mom ran over to me, and all I could say was, "no, no, no!"

My mom knelt down on the ground and asked, "what's the matter?" I could barely speak. I couldn't breathe. I finally said, "Kirby could be at the gas plant. We need to tell his mom and dad."

"I'll get Bud and Anna, let's pack up and get everything to the house," Mom said, "then we'll drive out to the plant."

When we got home, the details about the explosion were on the television, so we sat down and watched what the reporter was saying. I called Kirby's phone, but he didn't answer. He had been called to that gas plant many times. I prayed today wasn't one of them.

The reporter said there was a leak at the gas plant, and it started a fire. When they got the flames under control, they sent some men in to try to find the leak, and shut the valve off. They found the leak in a downstairs section within the hour, but it was too hot and too dangerous to try to fix. As the men started back up the stairs, there was another explosion. Two men got out, and one was trapped. An ambulance was in route, and everyone was moved out of the area.

As soon as they could get back in the building, they went in and brought the man out and put him in the ambulance. When the Chief of Police, Russell Allen, got to the scene and was told what happened, and who the victim was, it drove him to his knees, and he wept. He was a friend to the man and his family. Now he would be the bearer of this tragic news.

He stood up and told every man standing there, "Do not say his name until we notify his family. Take his body to the coroner's office, and wait."

While we were still watching the news, Brother Paul knocked on our door.

"Got time for a visit?" He asked, seemingly surprised that Bud had answered the door.

"Sure, Brother Paul, come on in," Bud said. "We're watching the television about the explosion."

"Got a cup of coffee coming," I yelled. "Have a seat. What brings you out this way today?"

There was another knock on the door.

"We're pretty popular today Mom," Bud said. "I'll get it."

But opened the door, and when I saw who it was, I put my arms around Bud, and said, "Come on in, stranger." Then something told me to have Bud sit beside me.

Bud leaned over and asked, "Who is it, Mom?"

"It's Russell Allen, the chief of police," I replied.

"Why is he here, Mom?"

Then I felt Brother Paul sit on the other side of me. Russell said, "There was a leak at the gas plant this morning. Kirby was called in to try to find it. He found it, but on his way out, there was another explosion, and he was killed."

Bud stood up, and Brother Paul pulled him back down. He went crazy screaming, "Not my dad! Not my dad! No, no, no!" He screamed and cried, until he could barely catch his breath.

I was in shock. I covered my mouth with my hands to muffle my cries. Bud finally got control of his emotions, and reached for me. He held me and kissed me as we grieved together.

The front door opened one more time. Kirby's parents, and mine, had received a call to come, but did not know why. The flood gates of tears and heartbreak were opened.

Brother Paul stood up as Fannie looked around the room and asked, "Where's Kirby?" Brother Paul said as he walked toward her, "There's been an accident."

Sim remarked, "I know, it's been all over the radio and television." Russell Allen looked at him, and he reached for Fannie as she fell to the floor. The sound of her screams was unbearable. Sim got down on the floor and held her.

Fannie looked up at Russell Allen and he said as he struggled to speak, "Kirby was killed in the explosion."

My parents, Guy and Jodie, stood there as if frozen in time. Jodie put her arms around Fannie while Guy tried to find words of comfort for Sim. Horror and disbelief had just rocked the world of this family.

Russell Allen explained to everyone what he knew. There were few answers at this time. He promised to keep the family updated as he got information. He hugged them, and then he left.

Brother Paul prayed for the family, and then he left. Jodie got up and put on a pot of coffee, that was all she could do at this point. Now would come the difficult task of planning Kirby's funeral.

Bud put his arms around me and asked, "What now?"

I responded, "We must make funeral arrangements for your father."

I wanted to scream, but it was all I could do to breathe. Death had taken the love of my life, and I wanted him back. I needed him, we needed him! My precious Bud, this terrible news has broken his heart and will forever change his life.

When our family left, Bud and I just sat on the couch. We were all alone and the shock was setting in. This house has never known such quietness as this moment.

Bud went to his room and closed the door. I got up and when I got to his door, I heard his cries. I didn't go in, I just put my ear close to the door and listened.

His words I could barely hear, but there was no denying his heartbreak! I gently cracked the door open, and what I saw made me cover my mouth so I wouldn't scream!

He was on his knees pouring his heart out to God. He kept asking, "Why," as he tried to catch his breath. I wanted to go in, but at that moment I knew that God was in control.

He got up from the floor and lay down on his bed. He turned toward the window, and I noticed something in his hand. Years ago, Kirby bought a set of walkie-talkies. He and Bud talked on them all the time.

I almost lost my mind as I watched him push the button and whisper, "Dad, can you hear me? I love you!" After a few seconds, he let go of the button and laid it down beside him.

I turned to walk away, but for some reason I turned and looked again. All of a sudden, the button on the walkie-talkie turned red, as if someone was responding!

"My God, My God," I thought. "Could it be?" I nodded my head, yes, and knew that all things were possible with God. I believe that Kirby was listening, and he was letting Bud know that he wasn't alone. I put my hands against the wall to steady myself and went to my bedroom.

I got undressed, put on my gown and robe and just stood there. I pulled the cover back and sat down on the bed. The moonlight shining through the window was the only light in the room.

I stood up to take off my robe and fell to my knees. There was a shadow in front of the window. I watched it move toward the door and then it was gone. My mind wouldn't allow me to sleep in this room. Too many memories and too much heartbreak.

I went to the living room and lay down on the couch. I was numb and afraid. What would we do without Kirby, he was everything to both of us? I just lay there talking to God, asking him how I bury a part of myself because that was what Kirby was. I cried and prayed until I fell asleep.

Sunlight shining through the window filled the room and woke me up. As I got up to walk to the kitchen, I saw Bud curled up in Kirby's chair covered up with his blanket. This was the only time in my life that I was thankful Bud couldn't see my face.

While I was pouring myself a cup of coffee, Bud walked in and said, "Pour me one, too, Mom." As I poured him a cup and sat it on the table, he sat down in his father's chair.

I put my arms around him, and as we cried together I said, "There are many things we have to do. We will be sad and it will be hard, but our love for your father will get us through it."

Bud cried until he couldn't catch his breath. I held him and said, "Death takes a long time to live with. We will hurt for a long time. We will miss Dad and it will be lonely, but God will watch over us, and so will your father. He will always be in our hearts."

Chapter Twelve

I called the funeral home and told them we would be there in a few hours. The director said, "Bring all life insurance policies and Kirby's clothes."

There was a wooden box in our closet where Kirby kept all important papers. I had never really looked at them. I found a policy for fifty thousand dollars.

Bud came in the room and sat down on the bed and asked, "Are we going to be able to make it without Dad?"

I was asking myself the same question. I took his trembling hand and said, "God will help us as He always has."

"I want to go to the funeral home," Bud remarked.

"You should be there," I told him. When we got to the funeral home, the director greeted us, then took us to a room. I gave him Kirby's clothes and the insurance policy.

Bud and I picked out everything. I described to him how the casket and everything that went with it looked. He was confused, but agreed.

I asked the director if Kirby's body was there, and if we could see him. The director looked at Bud and replied, "Now is not a good time. First thing in the morning would be better."

Bud never let go of my hand the whole time we were there. He was my rock, and I needed him to be strong. I was all he had left, and he was showing me that.

We left there and went to Ava Sue's Florist Shop to order flowers. I told Bud about everything that was about to happen so he wouldn't be confused. "There will be some people at the florist that will express their condolences. Some will hug you and some will shake your hand. This is all a part of love and respect for your father."

"Roses, Mom," Bud said. "Like the one bush that dad planted beside the house. He always laughed when I got stuck!" For a moment, there was a smile on his face.

When we got to Ava Sue's, people were there placing orders. Ava Sue took us in the back where we could have some privacy. The smell of all the flowers was incredible!

"Can we go home after this?" Bud asked.

I whispered, "That's our next stop." When we got in the car, Bud began to weep. I took his hand and held it tightly.

There were several cars at the house when we got there. People were bringing food and flowers. The phone was ringing off the wall, and I didn't know how many more times I could listen to the words, "I'm so sorry!"

"I'm going to my room." Bud said. "I can't take anymore!"

I called my mom and told her that I needed some help. Thirty minutes later, she walked through the door with an overnight bag and said, "Go lie down, I'll take care of things."

I closed the bedroom door and lay down on Kirby's side of the bed. I held his pillow in my arms wishing it was him. I cried until I was nauseated.

I fell asleep and woke up when Bud touched my arm and said, "Everyone's gone and Granny has supper ready." There was food covering the counter tops and my mom had started a list of everyone that brought food and flowers.

As the hours passed, I kept telling myself that I needed to find the strength to get through the next few days. Honestly, my grief wouldn't end in a few days, it was forever!

I tossed and turned all that night. The thought of burying the man I loved dominated my mind. I got up and went to the kitchen, and Bud was asleep, covered up in his father's recliner, again.

As I stood at the kitchen, tears ran down my face. I didn't know how I was going to say, good-bye. For a moment, just a moment, I sensed Kirby in the room. May be he wanted me to know that things would be ok. Maybe he was telling me, good-bye.

Goosebumps ran down my arm, but I wasn't afraid. The last two days had been hard and lonesome. I turned toward the table and there stood Bud. He was turning his head from side to side, and then he said, "I heard my dad's voice. I feel him in this room!" I put my arms around him and whispered, "I feel him, too!"

It was a beautiful, sunny morning. It was almost as if Kirby didn't want the sadness to overshadow our last good-bye. Bud and I got dressed, and I pinned a rose on his suit coat. He touched it and got a prick! "Thanks Mom!" He said.

When we got to the funeral home, Detective George was directing traffic. He and Kirby grew up together and were good friends. He came and opened my door, hugged Bud's neck and whispered, "I'll always be around if you need me."

Before we walked in the funeral home, I took a deep breath and told Bud to take my hand and be strong. My eyes flowed around the room. If there was a moment that I managed a smile this was it. The flowers and outpouring of love and support took my breath away. Ms. Ava Sue had outdone herself!

Brother Paul was standing inside the double doors waiting for us. He took us to a room in the back. Kirby's parents and mine were already there. The funeral director came in and said, "Let me know if you want the casket open or closed after the family viewing."

He rolled the casket in and closed the door behind him. Kirby's father opened the casket and wept. We all stood beside it with grief I couldn't have ever imagined.

Bud was holding my hand when I lost control of my emotions and began to cry. Then he asked me to put his hand on his father's hand. He held his hand up, and I guided it to his father's.

He lowered his cries and whispered, "I love you, Dad, and I will miss you. I will never forget the sound of your laughter, or the comforting touch of your hand. I saw a much greater man than anyone with their sight could ever see."

He pulled his hand back and said, "If my dad doesn't look like he did before the accident, please close his casket."

"Why would you request this?" I asked.

Barely able to speak he replied, "I want them to remember my dad like I remember him."

I explained to Bud what was going to happen during the service. Before the service starts, we will stand beside the casket and thank everyone that comes and pays their respects.

After two hours, the director sat us in the family section and the service began. Brother Paul started off with a prayer then spoke many things about Kirby and his life.

He stepped back and sat down, and then the song began to play. It was "Amazing Grace." All of a sudden, Bud stood up and began to sing. As if it were planned, most of the choir was sitting in the chapel. They stood and sang with Bud.

It was the most moving tribute I had ever seen. I could barely speak, but Bud found the courage to sing to his father. Brother Paul stood back up and said, "How can anyone compete with that!"

When the service was over, everyone left the chapel but us. I told Bud, "This is the last time to say good-bye."

I walked him up to the casket. He put his hands on it and barely able to say the words he whispered, "I love you,

Dad, and the next time we meet I'll be able to see your face."

The cemetery was about five miles outside of town, and I requested that only the family go to the graveside. When we got there and took our final walk, it still seemed so unreal.

"I never got to say good-bye and still at this moment I don't know how," I said as I put my head down.

Brother Paul said, "The Lord said, 'I am with you always.' And I say, the dark clouds will disappear. The sun will shine and love will find you, again."

I looked at Brother Paul and asked, "How do you let go of a part of yourself? That is what Kirby was to me!" I found it almost unbearable that I was burying the love of my life today.

I knew and believed that Kirby was in God's hands. Without warning my emotions took over, and I wept like a child. My mother stepped beside me, put her arms around me, and we wept together.

I couldn't watch Kirby's body be lowered into the ground so we walked over to a clump of shade trees. Few words were spoken, but many tears were shed.

When the grave was covered, we walked back over to it. Our parents said their good-byes and left Bud and I alone for a minute. I described all the beautiful flowers and how the grave looked.

We got down on our knees, and Bud touched the flowers. All of a sudden, he jerked his hand back, laughed and said, "That rose got me, Dad." His finger was bleeding from the thorn prick off the blanket of roses.

When we got up, Bud squeezed my hand, and said as he could get the words out, "I'll take care of you, Mom. It's my job now." As we walked out of the cemetery I took his hand and whispered, "I love you."

On the saddest day of my life, God found a way to bring beauty and compassion. God left me a part of Kirby, our son, Bud.

Chapter Thirteen

After a few weeks, I began to worry about Bud and the way he was dealing with his grief. He constantly sat in his father's recliner and at meals he sat in his father's chair instead of his. Maybe this was his way of holding on to his father's memory.

One morning as we were having breakfast, the phone rang. When I answered it, it was the plant manager of the gas plant. He wanted to have a meeting with me about signing off of some paper work.

I agreed to the meeting in two days. Not sure what was going on, so I called my parents and Kirby's parents and asked them to go with me. Kirby's father was a little reluctant to go in the building where Kirby died, but he said he would go.

The day of the meeting we were all curious. When we got there, another man was in the room, and he was introduced as their attorney. We all wondered why this attorney was here.

The plant manager said, "Under any circumstance of death in this building a settlement is always offered to the family."

Kirby's father stood up and in a rage yelled, "How do you put a value on a man's life? Do you know that his son is blind, and that his wife takes care of his son twenty four hours a day?"

The attorney stopped taking notes and said, "If you are uncomfortable discussing this maybe you should have a lawyer present. We are prepared to make an offer."

The room got quiet. Then I responded, "I think you're right. I'll contact an attorney, and he will contact you."

The plant manager said, "We are sorry for your loss. These types of circumstances are never easy."

Kirby's father looked at the plant manager with tears in his eyes and said, "I wish I had the courage to see where my son died, but I would never be able to forget it!"

We left and went back to the house. Sim suggested that I call Mr. Ted, a friend of the family, who was an attorney. I called him and told him what happened, and he said, "Let me make some calls, check some things out and I'll get back to you."

A week later, Mr. Ted called and asked us to come to his office. He wanted our parents there, too. Bud and I talked about what was going on and Bud asked if he could go, too. We all felt he should be there.

When we got to Mr. Ted's office, he took us to his conference room. He expressed his condolences, then said, "This is a very important matter. There is a lot at stake here for your family. When Kirby died, liability and responsibility was tied to the job site he was working at. In most cases a settlement is discussed and agreed upon. Kirby's age, and the needs of his family, will determine the amount.

"I would like to seek five million dollars in damages! Lifetime medical, dental and vision for you and Bud. Money will never make up for your loss, or bring Kirby back, but it will allow you to stay home and take care of Bud.

"There will be a separate settlement amount for Sim and Fannie. It's a lot to think about. I will submit a settlement offer, and I'll call you when they respond."

No one said a word. We just sat there in shock! As we got up to walk out, Bud took my arm and whispered, "We never needed money. I want my dad back!" I squeezed his hand and replied, "We'll talk when we get home."

I was in the kitchen cooking supper when Bud came in and wanted to talk. I told him he could ask me anything. He was worried that I might have to go to work to pay bills, and he would be with someone while I was gone.

"Your father and I have a savings account." I told him. "Everything we own is paid for. Don't you worry!"

Two weeks later, Mr. Ted called and said, "We could not reach an agreement so a court date has been set for two weeks. Don't worry, we might settle before then."

I thought, "How sad that when a tragedy happens a battle begins." I shook my head and covered my face. I didn't think that I could take anymore.

The next few days I wrote and mailed out thank you cards. I cried as I ran out of words to say. My days were consumed with sadness, and the thought that a hearing about Kirby's death would bring out things I was unprepared to hear.

A month later, at nine thirty in the morning, we went to court. When we got there Mr. Ted was waiting. He told us to all sit on the front row behind him.

As we looked around the courtroom, there were three attorneys at the other table, and several men sitting in the row behind them.

We all stood as the judge and court reporter came in the room. When everyone was seated the judge said, "This will be a hearing to try to get resolution. I've read all the briefs from both sides. I have the accident report and the financials from the company."

An attorney for the other side stood and asked to address the court. The judge replied, "I only want to hear from one person and that's Bud."

Bud and I stood up. We walked to the witness stand where he was sworn in and seated. Then I walked back to my seat.

The judge introduced himself and told Bud, "When I ask you a question, take your time and say everything you want to say."

Bud replied, "Yes sir."

Bud was on the witness stand for what seemed like an hour. They talked, they laughed, and when the judge excused him a tear was running down his face. I walked to the witness stand, took Bud's hand and led him back to our seats.

Bud turned back toward the judge and said, "Thank you, for letting me talk about my Dad."

The judge said as he stood, "You'll have my decision later this afternoon. I will inform your attorneys when I'm ready."

Mr. Ted told us to go to lunch and when we needed to come back he would call. As we were walking back to the court house Mr. Ted called and told us the judge was ready to read his decision.

The judge and court reporter came in and called us to order. He said, "It is the decision of this court that an award of five million dollars be awarded to Ruby and Bud. Lifetime insurance for Ruby and Bud. Sim and Fannie are awarded one million dollars. Arrangements for assets to be in place in thirty days. Court adjourned."

I was shaking so bad that I grabbed Bud's hand to steady myself. I stood up and hugged Mr. Ted's neck and said, "You'll never know how much you have done for us. We thank you."

Sim and Fannie invited everyone to their house for supper. I told them that we would be there, but we had a stop to make first. Bud and I went to the cemetery to visit Kirby's grave. We sat on the ground and told him everything.

It was a hot afternoon, and we were both sitting in the sunshine. Bud brushed his hand across the top of the grave. Unexpectedly, the wind blew up a cool breeze, ever so lightly. I couldn't help but smile, feeling he was watching over us.

Two weeks before Bud's birthday I met with Mr. Ted and some financial planners. Three accounts were set up. I had Mr. Ted draw up a trust in the event that something happened to me Bud would be taken care of.

Chapter Fourteen

Summer was coming to an end, and Bud would soon celebrate his sixteenth birthday. I asked him what he wanted and was shocked when he told me!

He replied, "I would like to go to the School for the Blind."

Caught off guard, I asked, "What brought this on?"

He told me he had been talking to Brother Paul and asking him to do some research and get information on a school close to home. "Don't be mad," he whispered. "At some point I will need to be able to work and live on my own."

I knew he was right, but I was unprepared for this conversation. I was impressed that Bud had taken it upon himself to get help with the research about school.

I went to see Brother Paul. He gave me an envelope full of information on two schools. That night Bud and I sat at the kitchen table and I read all the brochures to him. I saw the excitement on his face, and realized how important this was to him.

One of the schools was where I went to learn about blindness when Bud was first born. It was a two hour drive from our home and it cost fifty thousand dollars a year. Bud would live on campus and come home for holidays and summer break.

I took Bud's hand and said, "Let's take a road trip and check out the school!"

He almost jumped out of the chair and yelled, "Really Mom, really!"

Letting go was going to be hard for me. His happiness would make it tolerable. I called the school and made an appointment for us to visit on Saturday. Bud was on cloud nine for the next two days. I can't believe that I didn't think of this myself. Maybe I did, but didn't want to let him go!

We left early Saturday morning and talked all the way. Bud asked, "How did you feel when you went away to school?" I smiled and replied, "Probably the way you feel right now."

This school was way out in the country. As we pulled up the long drive, I saw several cottages that weren't there before, but for the most part, it was as I remembered it.

The grounds were beautiful. Lots of shade trees, benches and tables. There were students walking around with their canes, just laughing and talking.

When we walked inside, there stood Ms. Eleanor. She was just as I remembered her. A soft voice, kind face and she still smelled good today. I never forgot her perfume.

I was impressed that during our tour she defined everything to Bud. Every room was on the ground floor and three students lived in each section with a chaperone. Each student's room had a bathroom and a telephone.

This school was perfect, but I was scared to death. I knew this was something I had to do. Bud took my hand and asked, "Mom, please let me try it if only for a year?"

We went back to her office and did the paper work. With tears in my eyes, I wrote the check, and told Bud, "Ok, big boy, you're in!"

"School starts in two weeks," she said. "Your mom can visit every other week-end, and you go home on holidays and for summer break." The smile on his face was bigger than I had ever seen it!

When we got back home, I called both his grandparents and invited them over for dinner and to tell them the news. Everyone felt it was a good idea and they could talk to him every day and visit.

Bud shocked me when he took my hand and said, "You need to do something with your life while I'm at school. Maybe go back to teaching and we can spend summers together."

"Where did all your smartness come from," I asked.

He laughed and replied, "I had a good teacher!"

I climbed in bed that night and wept. I knew he wanted to do this, but selfishly it was hard to let him go. I was going to be alone and just taking care of myself was something I had never done.

The night before Bud left, I planned a family dinner. We shared laughter and tears. Bud promised to make us proud. After our family left, Bud and I loaded the car with everything he was taking. He had never lived around people other than his family. Could he adjust? We would see!

The drive was difficult for me. I didn't know how to let him go, or if I could. I was trusting strangers to take care of my son. What was I thinking? I took a deep breath and told myself, "I can always come back and get him!"

When we got to the school, Ms. Eleanor was waiting out front with two young men. She said, "Welcome, Bud, This is Eric and Chad. They are your room mates, and they will help you get your things to your room." Both boys touched Bud's arm and introduced themselves.

I thought to myself, "How can they help Bud when they're blind, too!" Chad told Bud how they have learned to count steps in certain areas and by doing so they don't need their canes.

It was time for me to leave. My faith and courage would no doubt be tested now! I hugged Bud so tight that I made him cough. He kissed me on both sides of my face and whispered, "I'll call you tonight. Drive safely, I love you!"

I had so much that I wanted to say, but I didn't. I yelled out, "I love you!" as he walked in the building and closed the door. I had a pity party for myself on the drive home. I felt terrible. I was scared and worried. I could hardly wait for his call tonight.

I drove to the cemetery before going home. I needed Kirby's strength and I always found peace when I was there. It was beginning to get dark so I walked back to my car. I wasn't paying attention where I was going and fell!

I reached up to grab hold of a headstone and a dove was sitting there. It didn't fly away or move we just looked at each other. Chills ran down my arms. I guess someone was watching over me.

Chapter Fifteen

I found it hard to do anything but wait on Bud's call. When he finally called, I could hear the excitement in his voice. He was talking so fast that I barely got to say anything.

He said, "Thanks, Mom, for letting me come here. It's amazing to be with other blind people!"

I heard something in the back ground and asked, "What's going on? Who is in there with you?"

"That's just the speaker system in my room. There's a music concert going on in the dining room, and I'm late. Gotta go Mom, I love you," he said as he hung up the phone.

I thought to myself, "Thank you, Lord, he hasn't been this happy or excited in a long time!"

It was quiet and lonesome at home without Bud. He was probably right when he told me I needed to get involved in something. Taking care of him left very little time for anything, but I loved it. Maybe it was time for me to go back to teaching.

Two weeks passed by quickly, and I was on my way to visit Bud. I wanted to see him for myself. I hoped that he was happy not just staying there to give me a break.

I pulled up and parked. Bud was sitting on a bench by the front door. As I got out he said, "It's about time Mom. I knew it was you because I could smell your perfume, and I always loved it!"

He held his arms out, and I walked right into them and gave him a big hug and kiss. He took me to the front door and opened it. I was amazed at that. Then we went to his room.

I asked, "How do you know which one is yours?" He squeezed my hand and replied, "Steps and counting, Mom. You taught me how to go room to room by counting my steps and remembering the feel of certain objects!"

His room was really nice. His stereo was on his desk with his books and tapes. His bathroom was really big and had a nice shower. His room was spotless! I was impressed!

The bell rang for lunch, so we went to the dining room. I remembered my first time in that room and what a disaster that was. Bud maneuvered around that buffet like it was nothing. Eric and Chad came over to say hello.

They told me how much they enjoyed having Bud as their roommate. Chad said, "You did a great job, Ms. Ruby. Bud is ahead of most of us in our class!"

Bud smiled and remarked, "My mom has been at my side all of my life. She is a teacher, but she put her career on hold for me." I felt good about Bud being here and having friends.

It was time for me to go back home. He hugged me and said, "Don't think you have to come every two weeks. They do things here all the time, and I want to fit in!" My feelings were hurt, but I knew I had to learn to let him go.

He was becoming his own man, and I had to step back and let life happen! Ms. Eleanor told me that she would call and keep me up to date on Bud and his progress, but from what she had seen so far, he was going to do fine.

Sunday when I went to church, Anna came up to me and said, "I really miss Bud. Is there any way I can call him?" I hugged her neck and replied, "Yes." I gave her his number and she smiled and whispered, "I'll call him tonight."

A few days later, Bud called and told me he had talked to Anna and really missed her. He told me all about the Halloween party that was coming up at the school, and how excited he was to bob for apples. Something he had never done!

Before we hung up, he told me that I could pick him up on the Tuesday before Thanksgiving. He wanted a big dinner with his grandparents and Anna if she could come.

I decided to surprise him so I invited Anna and her parents. Even though we were friends, I had never really had the chance to sit and talk with them. I would have the opportunity to learn about another disability. Anna's father, J.D., was deaf.

I couldn't wait to see Bud, but I was realizing more every day that he was happy at school, and I needed to stop feeling sorry for myself.

When I drove up to get him, he was still packing, so I took a minute to talk to Ms. Eleanor. She told me that Bud, Eric and Chad were almost inseparable!

"It's amazing to watch those three and the things they can pull off! Some of the things they do I didn't even think were possible. They have formed a band called, 'No Sight.' They play and sing every week-end at events and church on Sunday.

"Bud has mastered reading brail and is in the top of his class! He plays the piano and has a wonderful voice. Now, he plays the drums!

"Chad is just as smart, and he does sculptures from clay! You can't imagine! He allows us to sell them and use the money for the school. His work is always in demand. People find it hard to believe that a blind person can do this.

"Eric is a master at solving problems. Sometimes, he is one of our substitute teachers. The students really enjoy him, and he tells great jokes. He plays the guitar and is a wonderful cook!

"They are an inspiration to everyone here, especially me. I taught school for many years before I came here. I've been here twenty years, and I'm always amazed at what people with disabilities can do!"

On the drive home, I realized that in the short time Bud had been at school, he had grown and changed. Oh how I wish Kirby could see the man he's becoming.

Maybe he can!

When we pulled up the drive, Anna was sitting on the porch. Before I could get the car stopped, she was opening Bud's door. They hugged as if they had been apart for years! They sat on the porch and talked until dark.

Thanksgiving Day was wonderful. Our family was all there, and Anna came with her family. Other than speaking at church this was the first time I spent time with J.D. and Mary Helen.

After lunch, Bud and Anna decided to take a walk. All the men went out to the barn. Maybe to get away from the women! I didn't want to be rude, but I was curious to know how Mary Helen learned to deal with J.D.'s disability.

She told us how they met at a small college not far from here. "They offered two classes," she said. "Business, which was what I needed, and refrigeration, which J.D. needed.

"I had seen him several times, but every time I spoke all he did was nod his head. I was sitting outside with a friend one day when he walked by. I commented to her that he was rude because every time I spoke to him, he never spoke back.

"She laughed and said in a whisper, 'He's deaf.' I put my head down and felt like a fool. The next time I saw him, I walked up to him and tried to tell him I wanted to be his friend. He smiled, nodded his head yes, and walked away.

"The next day he walked up to me and handed me a Sign Language book. I said, 'Thank you.' Then he walked away.

"A week later, I was sitting on a bench, and J.D. came and sat down beside me. I had learned a few signs so we managed to have a short conversation. Over the next few weeks J.D. taught me a lot, but I wanted to learn more.

"Needless to say, I had a lot to learn because when I did some of the signs J.D. had a confused look on his face! I was interested so I wasn't giving up.

"I asked around to see if there was any sign language classes anywhere. I found one at the local hospital one night a week. I started going and met two other ladies. Our instructor wasn't too good, or visible, so we decided to form our own group and teach ourselves.

"Ms. Geraldine offered her kitchen table, so Nancy, who I call 'Sissy girl,' and I agreed to meet there once a week. Our classes became as difficult as challenging.

"You can just imagine three blondes, around a kitchen table believing we were experts! We laughed a lot and even made up signs of our own!

"Ms. Geraldine seemed to be the most serious and always studied. We gave her the title of our teacher. Nancy made us laugh because she was guilty of making up sentences that made no sense simply to have them for class.

"I loved to make up funny sentences. Most of all, loved to always say that the way they did their signs was wrong because I liked to argue!

"Not only did we learn and have a good time, we became very good friends. Maybe one day, our craziness would help someone. The key to sign language is the way you sign and your facial expressions.

"Just imagine three different opinions trying to figure it all out. The work was very difficult. Not only did we grow as friends, but we were learning to communicate without our voices.

"I never realized how tired someone's hands and arms get using them for every word. I couldn't imagine doing sign language for several hours, but that was the only way the deaf could talk.

"We laughed so hard sometimes at our mistakes. The faster we tried to sign, the worse it got. We wondered how to sign certain words that weren't in the book. Some of them were funny. Most of them were probably non-existent!

"Our biggest challenge would come if we were put in a situation to use what we had learned. For me, it could be an everyday language. I kinda liked J.D.

"When the weather was cool, we had class outside on Ms. Geraldine's patio. She had a beautiful garden in her back yard. It was shaded by huge trees with all kinds of flowers, pathways and benches. The perfect place to sit and take it all in.

"Pots and statues scattered throughout. Wind chimes and gourds hung in the trees. A place more beautiful than any magazine could describe. I would go to her house early sometimes just to walk through it.

"I had a ceramic rabbit that just sat on my porch. I decided to put it in the garden. I named her, 'Mags.' Ms. Geraldine put Mags in a wheel barrow full of plants along a pathway. Every time I looked at her I got a smile on my face knowing that she was a part of such a beautiful garden!

"Before long, J.D. and I were spending all our time together. Six months later, we were planning our wedding and a life together."

"What an incredible story!" I told Mary Helen. "I learn all the time that a disability should never define a person."

About that time, the men came back to the house and everyone was ready to go home and get a nap! Bud climbed in Kirby's recliner, and I stretched out on the couch. My heart was at peace. I finally realized that life for some families was simply different and that was ok.

Two days later, I took Bud back to school. My lonely days were coming back, but I was more accepting of him being gone. Anything that made his quality of life better was what needed to happen.

Chapter Sixteen

Bud continued to come home on holidays and summer break. Before I knew it, he was starting his last year of school and would graduate in nine months. Where did the time go?

He had grown to a young man. He was self-sufficient and the spitting image of his father. I was so proud of him, but there was a fear in the back of my mind that he would start his life away from home and me!

Two weeks after he was back at school, he called and said, "I've decided to get a seeing-eye dog! She has been trained and would be my constant companion. Her name is Tootie."

I didn't know if this was a good idea, or not, but if it made him happy I was ok with it. Then again, this could be a good thing! She would be with him all the time. "Tootie!" I like that.

Graduation was two weeks away. My parents and Kirby's parents were driving up with me. We were all excited. He was top of his class and would be giving the commencement speech!

We were sitting in the auditorium when they came in and took their seats. My heart was racing, and I cried. Bud took the stage and began to speak.

"I am sad to leave my school. My time here has been wonderful. I have learned to function as a blind person because of this school. I have made many friends and learned that a life is possible for people like me. I was privileged to come here, and I will miss all my friends.

"I am honored that my family is here today. I only wish that my father could be here, too. I intend to be the type of man that he would've been proud of, and I thank my mom, for being everything to me and for me."

Everyone stood and gave him a standing ovation! I was so proud! After the ceremony was over we all got together for lunch. Bud told us that he would be coming home in a few days.

I told him that I would come back and get him, but he asked if he could ride the bus home. He wanted to see how Tootie would do. I wasn't crazy about the idea, but that's what Tootie is in his life for.

It was almost dark and time for us to start back home. I told Bud to call me and let me know what day and time he and Tootie were coming home. I would pick them up at the station.

I hugged him and told him how proud I was of him. I didn't want to leave but I knew he was coming home forever! I liked the sound of that.

Bud called Thursday night and said, "We are leaving in the morning and should arrive in town at eleven thirty tomorrow morning. Can't wait to see you, and have you meet Tootie!"

I did the happy dance all through the house. "He's coming home!" I cried out. Then I picked up Kirby's picture, kissed it and said, "I hope you've been watching, and I know you are proud. I love you. He's become a wonderful man. Just like you."

Ms. Eleanor called this morning and told me that she had taken Bud and Tootie to the station, and they were waiting on the bus. "Try not to worry, Tootie is an incredible dog, and she will take care of him." She said.

PART
TWO

Chapter Seventeen

Ms. Eleanor sat with Tootie and I until it was time to get on the bus. She got my luggage and gave it to the bus driver. When it was time to board the bus, she hugged my neck and said, "Let Tootie do her job!"

I rubbed Tootie's head and said, "Get us on the bus. Let's go." When we got to the open door, Tootie stepped up and the bus driver said, "Three steps up, sir, and turn to your left. I will help you find a seat."

I replied, "Thank you."

I took the window seat and Tootie took the aisle seat. There was a lot of conversation going on so I figured the bus was full. When it pulled out, we moved from side to side. I thought, "This bus must be pretty big!"

It was a four hour ride until we got home. An hour later, the bus driver announced that we would be stopping for breakfast.

All of a sudden, I grabbed the arm of my seat. Something was changing. My normal darkness was getting lighter. What was happening? Was something wrong with my eyes?

My heart was racing! I sat very still. In an instant, I could see images of people. My eyes filled with tears. I couldn't believe what was happening! As quick as the images came, they were gone and the darkness was back.

I sat there not knowing what to do. All I could think was to stay calm. I put my arms around Tootie. The bus pulled into the café parking lot, and the driver said, "We'll be here an hour. Please be back in time."

I waited for the bus to empty. Then I stood up, and Tootie and I walked toward the front. The bus driver said, "Three steps down and you'll be on the ground."

I replied, "Thank you."

When I took the second step, a flash of light startled me, and I almost fell! I took the last step and just stood there. Within a second, for the first time in my life, I saw a huge light in the sky. It must be the sun!

I jerked back, and Tootie began to lick my hand sensing something was wrong. I rubbed her head and said, "I'm ok girl."

I heard a voice asking, "Sir, may I help you?" I smiled and replied, "No thank you, we've got it."

I stood there trying to catch my breath not knowing what was coming next. All of a sudden, I could see! I waited for the darkness to come back, but it didn't!

I walked Tootie over to a grassy area. I could barely contain my joy! I thought, "So this is what grass looks like." I wept uncontrollably! Tootie licked my face as I hugged and kissed her.

We went inside and ate breakfast. I took everything in, not knowing how long my sight would last. I looked down at Tootie, my best friend in the world. She was beautiful!

Her coat was very soft. I was told that she was black and now I know what that color looks like! Her chest was white and she has white on all four feet. Now I had seen several colors!

I kissed her nose and whispered, "Now girl, if I continue to see I will take care of you." I wasn't going to tell anyone about my sight until I was sure that the darkness was gone.

We got back on the bus, and I bowed my head and thanked God. The bus driver announced that we would be pulling in to our destination within the hour. I looked at everything and everyone! My neck was beginning to hurt from constantly turning my head, but I had to take it all in!

Suddenly, the darkness was back. I wanted to cry, but I prayed that my sight would come back again. As the bus pulled in to town, I could see once again. For the first time, I saw my home town!

I sat there looking from side to side. The bus driver touched me on my shoulder and asked, "Can I help you off, sir?"

"If you can get my luggage, my dog will do the rest." I replied. I rubbed Tootie's head and said, "Ok girl, let's get off this bus!"

As we got off the bus, I heard my mother's voice. I got goosebumps that ran down to my toes!

"Oh my God!" I thought. "Now I can see her face!" She ran up to me and took my hand. It was all I could do to breathe. She hugged me tightly, and when she let go we were face to face!

She was beautiful! Long blonde hair, blue eyes and a smile I couldn't get enough of. I put my hands on each side of her face, and kissed her as her tears were falling.

"I've waited for this day a long time," she whispered barely able to speak.

I took her hands and replied, "It's ok Mom, I'm home now."

I wanted to shout to the world that I could see, but I was afraid it wouldn't last. Mom took my hand and said, "Let's get to the car, and get you home."

I squeezed her hand and with a smile responded, "Mom, let Tootie and I show you what we can do. This is her job!"

"You're right son." She replied. "I did everything for you for so long that it's hard to stop."

"Tootie will amaze you." I told her. "She's trained to know and do everything for me. We've been inseparable for a year."

Mom stepped back and Tootie took the lead. I was blessed to watch my mom's reaction. She walked beside us and shook her head in disbelief! "Amazing," she whispered.

Then she asked, "Does Tootie want to drive?" As she laughed out loud. I thought to myself, "I do!"

Chapter Eighteen

As we drove through town, Mom did her usual and described everything to me. Little did she know that I was seeing it all for the first time. She said there were new traffic lights.

We came to a stop, and I looked up. Mom always said, "Red means stop and green means go." Wow! I thought, "That's what red looks like. I can't wait to see green!"

When Mom turned up the driveway, I said, "Stop Mom, I want to walk to the house with Tootie." She stopped, I opened the door, and we got out. She drove on and waited for us on the porch.

It was beautiful! Big Oak trees shaded the front porch. The house was white with green shutters and rocking chairs lined the front porch. When we got to the porch, I turned Tootie loose. Tears filled my eyes. It touched my heart watching her run for the first time.

My Tootie girl! How many times I wished I could see her. Thank you, God, she is amazing. When we went in the house, I took Tootie out of her harness because I knew my way around.

I almost lost control when I looked toward the fireplace and saw my father's picture. My back was to my mom because she was in the kitchen. I walked over to the mantel and found it impossible to take my eyes off of his picture.

I touched it with my hand and whispered, "I love you, Dad. I wish you were here." I touched my heart and said, "But you are always here." There was a wrapped gift box beside his picture, and my name was on it.

All of a sudden, my mom put her arms around me and cried as she said, "I'm so glad you're home. I have something for you." She put the gift box in my hand and told me that she wanted me to have it.

When I opened the box, I could feel it was a watch. Barely able to speak, she said, "It was your father's watch and now it is yours." It broke my heart, and I wept from the deepest part of my soul!

Coming home was more heart breaking than I had realized, but for me it was overwhelming joy!

"I just need time, Mom." I told her. "I love everything about being home, especially my memories of Dad."

She squeezed my hand and said, "Everything is set up for you in the bathroom. Get you a hot shower, then you and Tootie rest. I will call you when dinner is ready."

Now, the one moment I had waited for! I wanted to see my face! I opened the bedroom door, held my breath and walked toward the mirror. I covered my eyes with my hands that were sweaty and shaking.

Although I had touched my face a million times, I couldn't imagine what I looked like. I never stopped wondering!

I said in a whisper, "Oh God, I'll be happy with whatever face you have given me. Thank you, I can see it, if but once."

I pulled my hands back and opened my eyes. I was overjoyed! Blonde hair, sky blue eyes and perfect teeth and a nice nose. I touched my face and hair as I tried to control my emotions.

I cried to the point of barely catching my breath! Tootie rushed to my side. I looked at her and said, "It's ok." I didn't know how long my sight would last, but I wanted to see all that I could as long as I could.

I put my arms around Tootie and wept as she licked my tears. I held her so tightly that she got very still. For a year I have shared my secrets, my feelings and life with her. She has guided and protected me. I have never doubted her.

I kissed her nose and told her, "You will always be by my side. From now on, I will be your guide. I love you, Tootie girl!" I lay across the bed, and Tootie curled up beside me.

Tootie began to growl when Mom opened the door and said, "Supper is ready, come on." Mom surprised me when both sets of my grandparents were sitting at the table. We all hugged and cried.

Mom and my grandmothers put a spread on the table that almost made me hurt myself! It was good to be home. I sat there looking through my dark glasses at my grandparents for the first time. If only this could last forever!

We sat around and talked and laughed for hours. I saw the smiles on their faces and the tears in their eyes. I bet they were wondering what I was going to do now that I was home. I asked myself that question many times, but I still had no answer.

When they went home, Mom went to bed, and I went to my room. I went back to the mirror and just stood there. I couldn't get enough of looking at myself. I had two arms, two legs and a pretty nice body. I was hoping that the darkness wouldn't come back!

When I got in bed, I prayed, "Oh God, don't take these moments of my sight from me. I pray they last forever, but if they don't, I'm thankful for the ones you have given me."

Mom woke me up the next morning yelling, "Breakfast is ready! You and Tootie come on, or we'll be late for church!"

Mom took Tootie out in the backyard. When I got to the kitchen, she was fixing Tootie a plate. A smile came over my face and she asked, "What's that smile about?" I replied, "I can almost envision that you are spoiling Tootie like you do me!"

"She's a good girl!" Mom said, "Spoiled, a little over weight, but she's a part of our family."

I told Tootie to be a good girl, and that we would be back. We headed off to church. I was excited to see the people that I grew up around, but had never seen. I couldn't put a face with a name. I had my own way of knowing them.

While we were standing in the foyer, I heard a tapping sound coming closer and closer. I knew it was Mr. Pat and his walking cane. Then a familiar smell got to me. It was Ms. Jenny, I will never forget the smell of her soap.

Faces to names after all these years. I would have never imagined how they fit. As if it had never happened years of blindness were swept away. Not knowing for how long, yet thankful for every minute!

All of a sudden, a voice was yelling, "Welcome home, Bud. It's great to see you!" A beautiful young woman was running toward me. The voice told me that it was Anna. What a knock out she was! She jumped up in my arms and hugged me.

I couldn't take my eyes off of her. She had been my best friend. She was asking me questions so fast that I couldn't answer them all! Finally, she said, "Let,s do lunch and catch up." I smiled and replied, "Love to!"

Luck was on my side this morning as she sat in the row in front of us. I was hypnotized by her perfume and anxiously awaiting our lunch date. This was a great day. I put the faces to the people I had grown up with. I remembered their voices and some of their laughter.

Brother Paul announced that the church was having a picnic next Saturday. Anna turned around and asked, "Would you like to go to the picnic with me?"

"Sounds like fun!" I told her. Then she said, "I'll come and get you, and I'll be your guide for the day! See you Saturday," she said as we left church.

Without warning my mom leaned over and said, "Going on a date, are you! Let me tell you how pretty she looks this morning! Her hair is a beautiful shade of red. She has on a green dress that matches her eyes and her smile is mesmerizing!"

I nodded my head yes and smiled! I wanted to add, "You forgot to tell me about her beautiful legs!" Wouldn't that have blown her mind! And my cover!

Later that evening, Mom looked at the calendar and reminded me that I had an appointment to see my eye doctor. I thought to myself, "Maybe my sight is coming back permanently!" I hoped!

The morning we went for my check-up. I couldn't wait to tell him that my sight was coming back sometimes. I was normally there about two hours, so Mom would drop me off and come back later.

I was sitting in the chair when the doctor came in. We said our hellos. Then he took me to a room and began the usual examination. He pulled the machine back from my face and said, "Something has changed. The film around your eyes is shrinking. I've never seen this before!"

I put my hand on his arm and said, "I have on a blue shirt just like the one you're wearing!" He stood up and almost yelled when he asked, "Can you see? All the time?"

My voice quivered as I responded, "It started as flashes of light. Then moments of vision for a few days. I see all the time now, but I'm afraid to tell anyone, especially my mom, because the darkness might come back!"

"Keep a record," the doctor said. "When things begin to change, write it down. I won't tell your mother. Come back in two months. Incredible!"

I was sitting in the waiting room when Mom got back. She asked, "Any change?" I responded, "Very little."

I wanted to tell the world, but I was unsure how long I would be able to see. I hoped it would last forever, but nobody knows. I really wanted to tell my mom. If my sight continued until her birthday I would tell her. Her birthday was in about a week.

I felt ashamed that I hadn't already told her, but I knew the time was coming. She has never let me down and if I can trust anyone, it's her. I couldn't imagine how it would make her feel, even if it was only for a little while.

Chapter Nineteen

The next few days, all I could think about was spending time with Anna. Saturday morning came, and I was a nervous wreck. This was my first date. I hope she couldn't tell!

She knocked on the door, and I took a deep breath! "Come on in," Mom said. "I've fixed some food for y'all to take."

"Ready to go?" Anna asked. I responded, "Looking forward to it. Let's go!"

Anna told Mom that she would take good care of me, not to worry, but she didn't know what time we would be back. Mom took the food to Anna's car while Anna took my hand and walked with me.

When we got to the picnic area, Anna told me to wait while she found us a good spot and put the blanket and food down. I watched her walking back to the car smiling. As she opened the door she said, "Got us a great spot under a big old shade tree!"

There were a lot of people there. Everyone took a minute to say hello and welcome me back home. We sat down and Anna began to describe everything around us.

"Thank you, for describing the place we're at." I told her. She told me that I had always had a special place in her heart. It was because of her father, and she would like to tell me why. She began.

"My parents have had an incredible journey. My father was born deaf. His parents taught him sign language and how to read lips. Since he didn't attend her school, my mom and dad met at church, then again at college.

"They fell in love while they were away at school. My mom took it upon herself to learn sign language so they could talk to one another. She went to sign language classes at night and by the time they got married, they didn't need voices.

"My dad is a handsome man. He is tall, well built, has olive skin and beautiful brown eyes. My mom is a red head with green eyes. Sometimes she has an attitude, but a great outgoing personality!

"My dad got a job as the maintenance man at the church and my mom is a secretary. When I was five years old, my mom started teaching me how to sign. She told me it was a special way to talk to my dad.

"By the age of seven I was pretty good at it. I caught myself signing even if I was speaking. Habit I guess. I have never heard my father's voice, but he showed me what it looked like with his hands.

"Though the room was quiet, there were more words and laughter than anyone could imagine! The people at Calvary are wonderful to my dad. They gave him a job, and some even learned to sign so they could talk with him.

"Now, you know about my family, and I know about yours. Let's eat!"

She pulled two plates from her basket. When she took the foil off there was fried chicken, rolls, potato salad and deviled eggs. "My mom fixed this," she said. "I have put your plate in front of you, and to your right is a thermos of iced tea."

"Sounds wonderful!" I remarked. "I think my mom sent chocolate cake." I watched her reaction to me as we ate. Her kindness seemed genuine. More than I had hoped for, but then again, that was Anna.

After we ate, she said, "Take my arm and let's walk down to the lake and listen to the music." I thought, "This is working out just fine!" A Christian band performed for about two hours. They were really good, and we sang along.

I didn't want this evening to end. When the music stopped, Anna said, "Let's let the crowd clear out, and I'll take you home."

When we got back to my house, Mom was sitting on the porch. Anna helped me out of the car and walked me to the porch. She laughed as she remarked, "We had a great time and the cake was delicious! Most important, I got Bud back home in one piece!"

Anna hugged my neck and thanked me for going with her. Then she said, "Let's do this again some time."

"Anytime," I responded. "My date book is never full!" She threw her hand up in the air as she walked off then replied, "We might just have to fix that. Bye, bye!"

Mom and I went inside, she went to bed, and I took Tootie out back for a while. I laughed as she chased the fireflies. When we went to bed, I told her that I loved her and hoped that Anna would come to love her, too.

I couldn't go to sleep. I had Anna on my mind and the wonderful time we had today. I lay there remembering the time we spent together as children. We played together and spent every Sunday together at church.

A lot of kids made fun of us and said mean things. Two brothers, Jack and Jim, always laughed at Anna and said, "I'd rather be dead than red on the head!" She cried about their words many times.

Jack enjoyed tripping me as I walked down the aisle, and his favorite saying to me was, "One for the money, two for the show, that's right blind boy, there's no need for you to go!"

Then there was Joey. He was crippled from a disease called gout. It affected his hands and legs. Jack always called him, "Duck" because of the way he walked. Jack's favorite saying to him was, "Waddle for me crippled boy!"

Jack and Jim were always mean to someone. I always knew it was Jack because he had a strange laugh that sounded like a pig snorting. It always gave him away!

Their father owned the town's only bank. He was a kind man, unlike his two sons. Every time someone told on Jack and Jim, their father would punish them, but they always did it again!

One day Brother Paul gave them a lesson about the difference between Heaven and Hell. After that, they didn't bother us as much. "Thank you, Brother Paul," we thought.

The next thing I knew the sun was shining through my window, and Mom was yelling, "If you don't get up we'll be late for church!" I so wanted to tell her I was watching the sun come up, but not yet!

I sat up in bed and said to myself, "No way I'm going to miss seeing Anna! Forgive me Lord, you too!" We were almost late when we got to church. We took our seats, but I didn't see Anna.

I felt a hand on my shoulder. It was Anna and she asked, "Why don't you come and sit with our Sunday school class?"

Mom spoke up and said, "Good idea. Go and have fun!" We sat three rows in front of my mom. I told Anna I didn't want her sitting by herself. Anna looked back toward my mom and then she whispered, "Two other ladies are sitting with her."

As we sat beside each other I watched her and knew that she was someone I could trust. I closed my eyes and took a deep breath. Things were changing in my life, and I liked it.

Over the next few months Anna and I grew closer. I found it hard to imagine my life without her. After church, I asked Anna if she could do me a favor on Friday. "Sure, anything," she replied.

"My mom's birthday is Saturday. I need to go to the bank and get some money then shop for her a present." I told her.

"I'll pick you up at lunch, take you to the bank, and then we'll shop for your mom," Anna said with a smile.

I counted the days until Friday. Anna picked me up about eleven thirty. This would be a very special birthday because I was going to tell my mom that I could see. Would she understand, or be furious that I kept it from her? Then, what about Anna?

We were sitting in the lobby at the bank waiting for someone to help us when two masked men came through the door. "Everyone down on the floor," one of them yelled with a gun in the air.

Anna and I remained seated until one of them walked over to us, put his gun in my face and asked, "Are both of you hard of hearing?"

"Sir," Anna replied. "My friend is blind. I will help him get down on the floor if he must!"

"Leave him seated in the chair." He said. "You get over there with the rest of them!" I told Anna to do as he said, and I would be fine. Within a few minutes, they had taken all the money and were going out the door.

One of them stopped, turned around, walked toward me and said, "You're coming with us! The police won't put your life in danger!"

"Please don't hurt him," Anna yelled. "Take me instead!"

As he grabbed my arm, I fell out of the chair. He picked me up and I yelled to Anna, "Go to my house and tell my mother. Don't worry, I'll be ok!"

The other man said, "I'm going to get the van. Hurry and meet me out front!" I didn't make it easy for him to get me through the door, but when he did the other man yelled, "Come on, or we're going to get caught." He jumped out of the van, and they pushed me in the back.

I'm sure by now that someone had set off the alarm. All I could think about was how my mom was going to react! As we drove away I asked God to keep me safe.

The driver said, "We're not going to hurt you. Before long we'll put you out somewhere." Then he commented, "Must be tough being blind all your life." I had to wonder how he knew I had been blind all my life! Little did they know that I could see. Now all I needed was for them to take off their masks!

The guy in the passenger seat began to laugh and tell jokes about blind people. Something was familiar to me about this man. I remembered that laugh. I had grown up around it at church. I knew this man even though I have never seen his face. Little did he know that his payback was on the way if I got out of this alive.

"Why do you wear those dark glasses?" he asked.

I replied, "They keep me from looking directly in to bright light that could damage my eyes worse." All of a sudden, he leaned back toward me, pulled my glasses off, got in my face and whispered, "Be thankful you're blind. If you weren't you could be dead!" Then he put my glasses back on my face upside down as he laughed!

"He's blind, what an advantage for us. We can take our masks off! He'll never know who we are, and we don't need to be seen driving around with them on!" They took their masks off, and began to sing, "We're in the money!"

I was looking pure evil in the face. Two faces I would never forget!

After a while, the driver said, "I'm hungry. I'll pull in up here and get us a hamburger. Get me some money out of that bag!"

The driver asked me, "You hungry? Dinner is on you, I'm sure some of this money is yours!"

"I'm not hungry, but I could use a drink of water." I told him. I hoped this place had a camera at the drive through. If so this would be proof of their identity.

The driver handed the food to his partner and said, "Give me mine, I'm starving!" The man in the passenger seat picked up a bottle of water, removed the top and spit in it. Then he handed it to me and said, "Drink up!"

As he turned back around. I fumbled with the bottle and it fell in the floor board. I thought to myself, "You are one sick person!"

When they finished eating, the driver told his partner to divide up the money. It was getting dark, and I was worried about my mom and Anna.

We hadn't gone too far when the driver pulled off the highway and went up a gravel road. There was a sign that read private property. I could see an old cabin in the headlights and another vehicle. Now I was really worried!

The driver got out and went inside. A few minutes later, he came back and we left. As we were headed back out the driver said, "I got to pull over I'm getting sick!"

The other man replied, "Make it quick! I told you to go see your doctor. You've been sick for weeks!"

"My insurance only pays so much, and I'm already in debt, I've told you." As he fell to the ground, he could barely get back up and get himself in the van.

When we got back on the highway, I strained to see their faces when the head lights of the coming cars passed us. I was worried about what they would do to me. I pictured many things in my mind. At that moment I was glad they didn't know I could see!

I could see street lights ahead. I knew we were coming into a town. I was praying they would put me out and leave! The van came to a stop and immediately, I froze! The man in the driver's seat got out, opened the side door and said, "This is where you get out!"

He took me by my arm, pulled me out and threw me to the ground. He leaned down, looked me right in the eyes and said, "Today's your lucky day! Because you're blind, you get to live!"

Then he laughed that weird laugh, got back in the van, and as they drove away I managed to see the last three numbers of their tag, 550.

Tears filled my eyes as I thanked God that they didn't hurt me. I have never been so scared in all my life. Now I just wanted to go home.

I could see a building in the distance with their lights on. As I got closer to it, I could see it was a fire station. There was a man standing outside. As I got closer he asked, "Can I help you?"

"I need help," I said, as I managed to sit down on the bench by the door. He sat his cup of coffee down, looked at me and asked, "What happened?"

Before I could say another word he yelled out, "Stop! I know who you are. Your picture is all over the television!" He took my arm, led me inside and called the other firemen to the room.

"I'm ok," I said. "I just want to go home." One of the firemen told me that he had called the police and they were on their way. They fixed me something to eat, and the E.M.T. checked me out. I felt like a fool letting them think I was blind, but at this point I had no choice.

Within an hour, Russell Allen came through the door. He had been the Chief of Police for over twenty years. I expected my mom to be right behind him, but she wasn't. Smart move on his part!

I thanked all the firemen for all their help as the chief took me to his car. There were reporters outside, but I got right in the car and made no statement.

Before we got out of the driveway, Russell said, "Your mom has been going crazy. Take my cell phone and talk to her. I've already dialed the number."

I barely got out the word, "Mom," and she went crazy! All I kept saying was I'm ok and on my way home. Then I handed the phone back to Russell Allen.

For a moment, I wanted to scream! The worst was far from over. The truth was going to come out, and I didn't have a present for my mom's birthday. I couldn't help but wonder how my mom and Anna would react when they knew I could see.

I played it over and over in my mind how to tell her, and now saying it out loud makes it real. I never had an expectation of having my sight. Darkness was all I knew until now. It's a wonderful feeling not to be helpless!

If the darkness took control of my sight again, I could honestly say to God, "These moments you have given me have been enough."

When we got to the house, there was another car in the driveway. It was Brother Paul's. Anna came running out to the car and jumped in my arms. She was crying and shaking.

Before I stepped up on the porch, my mom had me in her arms. All she could say was, "I couldn't lose you, too!" After she settled down, we all sat in the living room and talked.

We all held hands and Brother Paul prayed. Russell Allen spoke up and said, "I'll be back in the morning and take a report of everything you can remember. Get some rest."

Tootie went crazy! She was licking me and barking! I told her that I was ok and then she settled down. Brother Paul left, and Mom gave Anna and I a few minutes alone.

She kissed me so quick that I couldn't keep my train of thought! I put my arms around her and kissed her back. We both laughed and I asked, "What took you so long!" She popped me on my shoulder and said, "I'll see you tomorrow!"

I took Tootie outside in the back yard, and we sat on the steps. I needed time to think and prepare for the consequences of my lie. I was ashamed, but telling this lie probably saved my life.

"Tomorrow," I told myself. "It all has to be told tomorrow."

Chapter Twenty

I woke up early the next morning, and as I walked in the kitchen my mom was sitting at the table drinking coffee.

"Happy Birthday!" I said as I hugged her neck and kissed her face.

"Thank you, sit down, and I'll pour you a cup."

I opened the back door and let Tootie out. I had prepared all night to tell my mom that I could see, but I still wasn't ready!

Mom fixed my plate and put one down for Tootie. I sat there very quiet, praying for the courage to do what I was about to do!

There was a knock on the door. It was Russell Allen and Brother Paul. Mom invited them in and I thought, "This is perfect! I'll tell them all at one time." When everyone had sat down I took a deep breath and stood up.

I walked over to my mom's chair, took her hand and said, "Something wonderful, yet scary has happened. I have been seeing flashes of light!"

My mom jumped up, held both of my hands and with tears in her eyes asked, "Can you see!" Brother Paul put his hands up in the air and shouted, "Thank you, God!"

"Sometimes, not all the time, and I never know when it's going to happen." I replied. Russell Allen shook his head, then he looked at me and asked, "Did you see the two men's faces?"

"Only a few times, but it was dark in the back of that van." I told him. "I don't know that I could identify their faces and be one hundred percent sure."

"I'm still optimistic!" Russell Allen said. "I'll send our sketch artist to the house." Then he asked, "Did they call one another by name?"

"No, but one of them had a familiar laugh to me. I remember a few things. They stopped to get something to eat and went through the drive through. The van was a dark blue. The last three numbers on the tag were 550. They pulled off and went up in the woods for a few minutes then got back on the highway.

"One of them said something I found very strange as he divided up the money. He said, "Thanks Dad."

Russell Allen said, "For now, none of this information will be released. Maybe it's a good idea that everyone continue to think that you're blind. The robbers might come back, or they might live here. Keep your secret a little while longer. I'm headed to the bank, we'll talk later!"

I looked at my mom and said, "I wanted to tell you, but I was afraid to get your hopes up. I didn't know how long my sight would stay. Happy birthday, and I love you!"

As tears ran down her face she smiled and said, "I understand your fears and I'm glad I know, now. My birthday dinner is on you!"

"You pick where you want to go, and I'll be glad to pay!"

Russell Allen called later and told us that he got statements from the bank employees. They described the two men as wearing masks and gloves. One of them had a gun. The other one carried a bag. He emptied all the cash drawers, but never touched the safe.

The bank didn't get a pick up this week so there was more than usual, about fifty thousand dollars. The bank's owner, Mr. Bill, was turning over the surveillance tape. He also said, "My son filed a police report the night before the robbery that a blue van had been stolen from his car lot."

Russell Allen said, "I couldn't help but think how interesting that story was. Before I could get back to my car, a call came in asking me to come back to the station. A police chief from another county said he had found a van that had been set on fire on the side of the road. Maybe it was the one the kidnappers used.

"I told him that I would ride down there with him and look at it. That's all I know now. I will stay in touch." Then he hung up.

When I got off the phone, Mom asked me, "When are you going to tell Anna, or are you?"

I covered my face and broke out in a sweat. "I will tell her when all this police business is finished. I need to be sure that she is safe. I hope she will understand and forgive me."

Mom and I celebrated her birthday at the catfish buffet. It was really good, but I missed Anna being with us. But this was my mom's day! I called Anna when we got home, and invited her over for lunch after church.

Anna and I spent our Sunday talking about my kidnapping. She had a million questions, but I couldn't give her any answers. I had to keep quiet about everything. Especially my sight.

When she left that evening, I told my mom that maybe Russell Allen would get some news about these guys soon and then I could tell Anna everything.

Monday morning, I was on the porch when a motorcycle came up the driveway. Mom stepped out the door and commented, "Surely, y'all are not going on that thing!"

Russell Allen laughed and said, "This is my day to chauffeur the blind man, and this is what I like to drive!"

I thought to myself, "This is going to be cool!"

Then Russell said, "Maybe Bud will remember some things. His view would be somewhat blocked in a car. Fresh air always clears my mind."

Wasn't long before we were coming into a small town. We saw several small cafes, went in and asked if they had any type of surveillance, and they all said, "No."

We did that two more times and finally we found a barbeque place with a drive through. Russell Allen went in and asked if they had surveillance cameras. The man told him, yes, because he had been robbed twice.

He gave Russell Allen the tape and told him if there was nothing on it he needed to please send it back. Russell Allen looked at me and said, "If we could find that gravel road, we might be able to get some more answers."

We met with the other Chief of Police and looked at the burnt van. There was no evidence to be found, but they were sending pieces of the van to the State crime lab and if anything showed up he would let Russell Allen know. We left and got back on the road.

We hadn't gone far when something caught my eye, but Russell Allen was going so fast that I didn't have time to remember!

"If you would slow down!" I told him. "Stop, stop, go back! That road back there had a private property sign and it was beside a gravel road."

We turned around, and when we got back to the road, Russell Allen said, "It's dangerous for us to go up this road on my motorcycle. Someone could be up there and hear us coming. Let's hide the bike in the woods and walk up the road."

We hid the bike about one hundred feet up in the woods and quietly walked up the road. We were both nervous and hoped we didn't get caught. We could see nothing but trees. Then all of a sudden, we were in a clearing and saw an old cabin up on a hill.

We walked along the tree line just in case someone was up there. We made our way to the cabin and walked around back. There were green plants, about six feet tall as far as the eye could see!

Russell Allen grabbed my arm and said, "Stop! This is a marihuana field. We've got to get out of here. If we get caught up in here, we will be in serious trouble. I don't have my gun, or a radio."

Before he finished telling me how stupid he was for not carrying his gun, we heard vehicles coming up the drive. Russell Allen yelled, "Run, run into the field!"

We ran for what seemed like ten minutes. We got separated a few times, but we ended up at the river bank at the same time. As we stood there figuring out what to do. Voices were getting closer and a dog was barking, too!

I looked at Russell Allen and said, "I can't swim!"

He replied, "We need to get in the water so that dog can't pick up our scent." When he stepped off in the water, it was over his head. He pulled himself back up on the bank. Looking from side to side, he said, "We've got to hide, they're getting closer. If that dog comes after us, you're going to learn to swim, or drown!"

Fear set in as our options became few. Not only did we hear their voices getting closer, a barking dog and now we could hear boats coming. There was an old wooden boat turned upside down on the bank.

We decided to hide under the boat because there was no time to run! We turned it up on one side. He climbed under one end and I got under the other end. Then we pulled the boat back over us.

The smell of dead fish under that boat was stifling! That wasn't even the worst. There was a wasp nest under there somewhere, and they were stinging the fool out of us. It was hard not to yell!

Their voices were right on top of us. Apparently, they were loading the boats with marihuana and taking it down the river. Finally, the boats left and their voices got quiet as they walked away.

I slowly raised one end of the boat up, and two of the men were standing by the edge of the water. One of them said, "Now that the work is done. I think I'll take the old boat out and do some fishing."

He started to turn the boat over when the other man said, "Why use that old thing. This one is much better and it has a motor."

"Give me a minute," The man standing beside the old boat said. "I gotta use the bathroom!" It was all I could do from laughing out loud. He was up at Russell Allen's end of the boat!

We could hear the sound of him urinating on top of the boat. It was running on us through the cracks! We heard the boat pull away. We waited a few minutes then we raised the boat up and got out.

We were slapping ourselves all over! There were wasps all over both of us, and they were still stinging! The stench of urine and the stings from the wasp drove us straight to the water.

Russell Allen said, "We've got to get out of here. Let's find our way back through the field and get to my motorcycle." We crept low and slow through the field. I wiped the sweat from my face on my shirt sleeve. The air was so hot among the plants that it almost seemed to burn my face.

The deeper we crawled in the field, the more I felt uneasy. When we got back to the edge of the field, we turned and ran for the woods. We walked quickly, bracing ourselves against the trees.

We were about ten feet from the motorcycle when Russell Allen grabbed my arm and yelled, "Stop!" He pointed to the back tire of the motorcycle, and a huge snake was coiled up by the back tire watching us!

I whispered, "Can this day get any worse!"

Russell Allen said, "We've got to find some way to make that snake move, but not in our direction!" We backed up and found some sticks and rocks. We turned back toward the snake, and it was gone!

I threw rocks on both side of the back tires hoping if it was still there, it would move. We both looked up at the same time and said, "Thank you, Lord!"

We started pushing the motorcycle back to the road, and bad luck found us again. We were in the middle of a briar patch! We couldn't stop, or backup, we had to keep going.

It wasn't enough that we smelled like urine and were covered in wasp stings. The briars ripped our pants and cut us everywhere they touched us.

When we got to the road, Russell Allen poured the power to that motorcycle, and we were gone! I held on for my life. He must have been going one hundred miles an hour. We broke every speed limit and almost wrecked twice before we got to the next town.

We drove around to the back of a small café, parked and went in to get something to drink and steady our nerves. We got a table in the back and just sat there. Russell Allen put his head down and said, "This is big, really big! We're lucky we got out alive!"

We decided to get back home because someone could have seen us and followed us. When we got back to my house, my mom was waiting on the porch.

Mom looked at us and asked, "What happened to you guys and what's that smell?"

I told her how our day had gone and showed her my wasp stings! She began to laugh, but we found no humor in it! She stood up to go in the house and said, "I'll get something for those wasp stings and chiggers, too!"

When she got back to the porch and she doctored us up, I looked at Russell Allen and said, "No more road trips with you!"

Russell Allen stood up, and as he walked off the porch he said, "I'll start getting my notes together, and we'll talk in a few days."

Mom told me to come on in, that she had run me a tub of water and put some oatmeal bath beads in it. It's supposed to help sooth itching. I was willing to try anything at this point! I soaked for about thirty minutes, dried off and it did stop some of the itching.

When I walked in the living room, she was sitting on the couch laughing. She held up four different colors of fingernail polish and asked, "Which color do you want?"

I looked at her and before I could say anything she said, "In the old days, people put fingernail polish on chigger bites and it stopped the itching!"

I laughed until I almost lost my breath and managed to say, "Red!"

"Anna has called twice today," she remarked. "She asked me what you were doing on the back of a motorcycle!"

As soon as I stopped using both of my hands to scratch myself, I called her back. She must have asked me ten questions before I got "hello" out of my mouth.

I told her that I had always wanted to ride on a motorcycle and the opportunity came along. Needless to say, that wasn't the explanation she was looking for. I asked her out to dinner tomorrow night to explain everything.

She replied, "I'll pick you up at five thirty. If your explanation is not to my liking, you can walk home!" Then she laughed and said, "See you tomorrow."

I hung up the phone and went to my room. Tootie was stretched out across the foot of my bed. I kissed her on the nose and whispered, "I am happier than I have ever been in my life. You are one of the reasons why! I love you, Tootie girl, good night."

Anna picked me up and wasn't very talkative. I felt she was somewhat mad at me. When we got seated at our table, she said, "Help me understand why you would risk your safety on the back of that motorcycle?"

I had rehearsed all night the things I would tell her and why. I took my glasses off and looked at her and said, "There is only one way to say this. My sight has been coming to me in bits and pieces!"

As tears ran down her cheeks she replied, "That's a miracle! How often does it happen? Can you see me now?"

"Yes," I answered. "You are so beautiful! I have been looking at you for weeks."

She slammed her hand down on the table and yelled, "Weeks!"

"Please let me explain," I asked her. About that time our food arrived, and she took a minute to calm down.

I explained to her about the flashes of light, but that the darkness always returned. I never knew when, or for how long a period of time, I would be able to see. Her facial expressions begin to change as if she understood.

Quickly, she covered her mouth with her hand and said, "You saw many things that happened during that bank robbery. That's why you were on that motorcycle with Russell Allen!"

"Yes, I did see some things, but most important, I saw their faces because they took their masks off thinking I was blind!" I confessed. I continued to tell the story, and explained that no one must know about my sight. "Those men could come after me, or my mom, and now you!"

I scratched my head as I told her that something about one of those men was familiar to me. It was his laugh, and I'd heard it before. I told her the rest of the story about mine and Russell Allen's day. If we keep my sight a secret, maybe I can help catch these guys.

Anna smiled and said, "I won't tell anyone." Then she leaned across the table, kissed my face and whispered, "It's a miracle!"

After lunch, we got in her car and she asked if I wanted to take a drive. We drove out of town, and she pulled over and asked, "Would you like to drive?"

When I said, "Yes!" I think I screamed it!

We changed seats, and I reminded her that I had never driven before! My heart was racing so fast that it was hard to catch my breath. She took my hand and said, "Take your time, we'll be fine."

The smile on my face said it all! After a few minutes, I seemed to have it under control. I was driving very slowly but it was terrific! After a while, we switched seats, and she took me home.

"How can I ever thank you for today?" I asked. "It's been one of the greatest days of my life!"

She replied with a smile, "let's make sure it's not one of the last."

When we got back to my house, Mom was sitting on the porch. Anna let me out and didn't walk me to the porch. Mom looked at me and remarked, "You must have told her, and she understood."

"She's an incredible woman, and I really like her," I said. "I'll tell you a secret! She let me drive her car today. Incredible!"

I gave her a thumbs up, and said, "It's Tootie time now."

Chapter Twenty-One

Russell Allen came to the house the next morning. He suggested that I continue to let everyone think I was blind, hoping the two robbers would feel safe and show themselves again. It was scary, but exciting to be a part of this!

He also told us that the marihuana field was under surveillance, but the county where it was located had to do the investigation. Mom wrote down everything I told her, and I described the two men as best I could.

Mom commented that I needed to go back to school! She was right. I needed to learn to read and write. Something that wasn't relevant when I was blind. She smiled and said, "I'll teach you how."

For the next couple of weeks, Mom taught me during the day, and Anna and I saw each other every evening.

One beautiful sunny day I decided to take Tootie on a walk. My mom had pulled me in my wagon up and down that road a million times when I was a child. I wanted to see it for the first time!

Mom yelled out, "If you wait I'll go with you."

"We got it, Mom!" I replied. "You taught me who and where our neighbors were before I was six years old. Tootie will be with me. We'll be fine!"

For the first time, I could walk and see the things that my mom described to me as a child. Come to think of it, I wondered where my wagon was!

I hooked Tootie up in her harness, and when we got to the end of the driveway, we took a left. That would take us by Mr. John's farm. My mom described it so many times that I couldn't wait to see it for myself.

I knew we were close because I could see his goats and hear the dogs barking. I remember speaking with Mr. John many times, but there was one time I couldn't forget. He was a soft spoken man. He always patted me on my head until I was big enough to shake his hand.

He wasn't just a farmer, he was also a teacher. He would always stop his work and talk to us when we went by his house. One day when we were going by the fence, Mr. John yelled out, "Wait up Bud! I've got a surprise for you!"

Mom pulled the wagon to the gate, and Mr. John said, "Hold out your hand. I want you to meet my prize goat, Mr. Sippi! He's going to a new home in Texas!"

I was so excited that I held out both hands. He placed my hands on Mr. Sippi's side and let me rub him all over. I hope the smile on my face let Mr. John know that was one of the greatest moments of my life.

I told Mr. John, "What a great name, Mr. Sippi, for your prize goat! Do you have other animals, Mr. John?"

He told me that he had a dog named Gracie. She stayed in his house and loved to lay on her back with her belly looking up at him. He had two other dogs that stayed outside and worked with his goats. Paradine was a great guard dog. Kara was yellow and white and had incredible instincts. He also had chickens and a miniature horse.

I thanked him for telling me about his farm, and for letting me rub Mr. Sippi.

Tootie and I turned and started the other direction. The next house we got to always made me hungry! Ms. Patricia lived there.

She owned a catering business. The smell coming from her house was wonderful. She attended Calvary Church and sometimes sat with us. She had a beautiful smile and was very kind.

One day at church she said, "One day when you come by my house, I am going to have a surprise for you."

I whispered back, "Thank you, my favorite is chocolate!"

A few days after that, Mom was pulling me in the wagon and she stopped quickly. She said, "There is a table at the end of Ms. Patricia's driveway. There's a sack on the table with your name on it!"

"Oh, oh, Mom!" I yelled. "Open the sack, and I hope it's chocolate!"

My mom laughed and said, "Yep, but there's more than one in there!"

I begged her to let me have just one bite, and I would eat the rest when we got back home. She would put the cupcake in my hand, and I would smell it until I couldn't take any more breath in.

Then I would take a big bite! All I could say was wonderful, but it didn't sound like that with my mouth full. Ms. Patricia must have left me cupcakes a hundred times. What a great lady! Good cook, too!

The closer we got to her house, the more prevalent that old familiar smell became. When we got to her driveway, I stopped and tears filled my eyes. The table had been put back out and there was a sack with my name on it!

I picked it up and not only was my name on it, but it also said, "Welcome home!" I looked at Tootie and her nose was up in the air. She smelled it too! When I opened the bag, there were three chocolates and one plain. How kind of Ms. Patricia, knowing that dogs aren't supposed to eat chocolate.

I told Tootie, "Let me have a bite, and then you can have one!" After we did our sampling, we turned and went back home. I had to hold the bag up in the air because Tootie wanted them all!

Mom was sitting on the porch when we got back. Before she could ask any questions I said, "Look what we found," and held the bag up.

I saw the smile on my mother's face. I think it touched her heart when people showed me love and compassion. I looked at her and said, "I can't let this good stuff go to waste. One for you, one for Tootie and two for me!"

Mom said as she laughed, "Just make sure I don't get the one that has a bite out of it!"

The next morning, Mom began teaching me how to read and write. It seemed a lot harder than brail, but it was incredible to finally see a picture of what some of these words looked like.

Russell Allen came by a few hours later to give us an update. Mom was helping me by writing down everything I could remember about the day of my kidnapping.

He also reminded me to continue to let everyone think I was blind. He also said, "When we have enough evidence, the charges will be made. Your secret will be kept until they are caught and in custody."

It was scary, but exciting to be a part of this. Who knows! These guys could be long gone.

Anna called and wanted me to go with her to look at a new car. This was going to be fun! How often does a blind man get to help pick out a car? I see the humor in it!

As we walked up and down the rows of cars, a salesman came out and asked if he could help us. Anna said, "I'm just looking, but if I see something I like I'll let you know."

All of a sudden, another man walked up behind him and scared him! They both began to laugh. I stood there holding my breath and couldn't move!

I took Anna's hand, pulled her close to me and whispered, "I remember that laugh, and they look like the two men driving the van!"

Anna quickly told them she didn't see anything she liked so we left. When we got in her car, my hands were shaking! She said, "This is unbelievable! Those two guys are Jack and Jim!"

One of the town's cafés was right next door so we pulled in to eat and talk about what just happened. We got a table on the patio and Anna asked, "Are you sure it was them?"

All I could say was, "I'm pretty sure about their faces, but I'm positive about that laugh!" We ordered lunch and as we waited on our food we realized that from where we were sitting, we could see the side and rear doors of the car lot.

If I was right that Jack and Jim kidnapped me and robbed their own father's bank, my long awaited justice was coming! Being a part of this was exciting, but I also knew it was dangerous.

"I have a great idea!" I told Anna. "I could come here often and watch who comes and goes at that car lot. Maybe even video it and give the information to Russell Allen."

"You could get yourself hurt, too!" she replied.

When I got home, I called Russell Allen and told him my plan. He thought it was a good idea and asked me to keep him updated.

Tootie and I had lunch at the café every day for a week. Every other day four men came with a load of boxes and took them in the back door of the car lot. "Perfect set-up," I thought. "Great place to hide the marihuana and vehicles to transport it."

The next morning, when Mom and I got to church, Anna was waiting for me in the lobby. She told me that Joey had been asking about me, and he was sitting down front so we walked down to where he was sitting.

I was glad I had my glasses on because it broke my heart to see what gout had done to his body. I held out my hand and said, "Hey man, it's good to be able to talk to you!"

He moved over and I sat down beside him. We talked a few minutes and when the music started I said, "Come see me at my house sometime." Then Anna and I went back up to where my mom was sitting. Ms. Patricia was sitting beside her so Anna and I sat in front of them.

I turned around and told Ms. Patricia how much I appreciated the cupcakes and the welcome home. Before the service ended, Brother Paul asked Jack and his wife to come down front. He announced to the congregation that Jack had bone cancer and needed a bone marrow transplant.

For a moment, just a moment, I felt like Jack was getting what he deserved. I felt that this was payback for what he had done to me, Joey, Anna and others, too!

He also said that the family was asking for our prayers and anyone willing to be tested to see if a match could be found. Then I felt sorry for Jack, and especially for his family. There was much more coming that they knew nothing about!

The one thing I could say for sure was that Jack and Jim were nothing like their father. He was a very kind man and smart, too. He owned the only bank in town.

As we all walked out into the foyer, Mom took my hand and said, "Wait a minute, I'm signing up to be tested." I squeezed her hand and replied, "This surgery could be dangerous, and he's never done anything for you!"

"It's not about him so much as it is about what God puts on your heart. What if that were you?" she said softly.

"She's right," I told myself. "I may have problems, but I'm not fighting for my life. Sign me up, too." Then the old devil got back in my mind, and I thought, "Wouldn't it be something if I, the one he picked on all the time, were to be a match!"

We walked out of church and Mom hugged me and whispered, "I'm so proud of you. It's ok to be mad, but this is life or death for Jack."

After lunch, Mom, Tootie and I were sitting on the porch when a car came up the drive. It was Joey. When he got out, Tootie ran up to him and gave him a kiss. Then he walked up on the porch and sat down.

Mom said, "I'll let you two visit. I need to clean up the kitchen.'

"Today was a shocker, wasn't it!" Joey said. "Justice has come, and I hope he feels every minute of it!" I sat there and let him vent years of hidden anger. I knew how much he wanted revenge after he told me stories that I never knew. His mind was consumed with revenge!

At that moment, I felt sorry for Jack and Joey, but for some reason I wasn't feeling sorry for myself. Little did Joey know that Jack was facing a possible double death sentence. If the cancer didn't kill him, a life in prison might!

Joey stood up and said, "I better go. I have to go to work early in the morning. I'd like to visit you again sometime."

"Anytime, don't be a stranger." I told him. "Maybe we can have lunch one day."

I took Tootie in and went to my room. I sat on the bed and cried. How terrible Joey's life had been at the hands of Jack. I wasn't so sure that Jack deserved to breath the same air I do, but that's God's call, not mine. Vengeance belongs to the Lord.

I woke up to the smell of bacon frying. It was a race between me and Tootie to see who got to the kitchen first! I lost! I let Tootie out and sat down at the table. Mom said, "I couldn't help but overhear Joey's story yesterday." She put her arms around me and said, "God has enough second chances to go around! Maybe together, you and Joey can find a way to forgive Jack."

For the next few days, Mom and I worked on my reading and writing. I wanted to take Joey to lunch, so Mom took me to the courthouse and dropped me off.

I finally found Joey and asked him to lunch. He said, "Give me about fifteen minutes, and I can go." He told me what his job consisted of, and how much he liked it. "The best part!" he said. "I know what's going on in this town before most people do." Then he looked at me.

Our conversation during lunch was mainly about Jack and Jim. He told me that something big was about to happen that would shake up the town, but he couldn't talk about it. Then he got a big smile on his face!

When lunch was over, and we got back to the courthouse, I walked across the street to talk to Russell Allen. Fear began to set in as I wondered what repercussions would come for me and my mom when I testified.

Russell Allen assured me that I would be invisible and a protected source until it was time to testify. I had a good feeling about getting my revenge on Jack and Jim, but if they weren't found guilty, what then?

Surely, Russell Allen had this process down to a science! He called my mom and told her that he was bringing me home. She said, "Great, I have some errands to do, but I won't be gone long."

Later that afternoon, I was sitting out on the porch with Tootie enjoying the warm sunshine on my face when everything went dark! My sight was gone and the darkness was back!

I grabbed the arms of the rocking chair and tried not to scream! My heart was racing, and I could barely breathe. My mom drove up and yelled out, "Come and help me unload the car!"

As she got to the porch, she knew something was wrong. "It's back Mom, it's back!" was all I could say.

She sat the bag down, took my hand and calmly said, "Relax and try to calm down. Maybe all this stress has caused a problem. It could be from the sun because your eyes are not use to that kind of light."

I squeezed her hand and replied, "You could be right." Then Tootie and I got up and went inside. Mom went back to unload the car, and before she finished my sight was back!

"We're going to see your doctor!" she said. "Something is changing. Maybe not forever, but at least for now." She called and got me an appointment for the next day. I wanted some answers, but I didn't want to hear the word, temporary!

The drive to the doctor's office made me nervous. As we sat in the room waiting for the doctor, I didn't know what to expect. He came in and did several tests, and then we waited for the results.

When he came back in the room, he shook his head and said, "The film covering your eyes is still shrinking. It could stop at any time, or completely go away. Everything else is normal and the same as it was."

When he walked out and closed the door, Mom and I just sat there. Mom took my hand and said, "Enjoy every moment. Take nothing for granted!"

There was never going to be a moment in my life that I could say my sight would be permanent. Having it was a miracle, losing it would be devastation, for me!

Chapter Twenty-Two

That night, Brother Paul and Anna were invited for supper. As soon as we finished, the phone rang. Mom answered it and handed it to me. It was a doctor at the hospital and he said, "Your bone marrow is a match for Jack. If you're still willing to be a donor, we'll schedule the procedure in four days."

I sat there in shock, thinking, this is true justice! Without me, he was in serious trouble! I replied, "Yes," then he told me he was going to inform the family.

I handed Mom the phone and then told all of them that I was a donor match for Jack! I put my head down and covered my face. I was humbled. Not only was God giving me a miracle, but allowing me to give one, too!

Brother Paul put his hand on my shoulder and said, "When God gets involved, wonderful and miraculous things happen!"

Jack and his family would be told about the match in the morning, but I insisted that I remain anonymous. Surgery would be in four days.

When Brother Paul and Anna left, Mom, Tootie and I went and sat on the front porch. The moon was as yellow as a lemon. There was a warm, light breeze blowing and the stars were putting on a light show.

Tootie began jumping around, chasing lightning bugs. Mom and I laughed at the simplicity of a summer's evening on the porch. Mom stood up and said, "God has given you a miracle to pass on to Jack. He has a reason for everything!" Then she kissed my face and said, "Good-night."

Sunday morning at church, Brother Paul announced that a match for Jack had been found. The donor wanted to remain anonymous and surgery would be in two days. Mom and Anna squeezed my hands at the same time. My heart was pounding, and I was scared.

Monday morning came, and I was packing my bag for the hospital. Mom came in and said, "I need to go visit a sick friend and let her know that I won't see her for a few days."

I replied, "Ok mom, be careful."

I had just finished packing my bag when someone knocked on the door. I thought it was Anna. When I opened it, there stood Jack and Jim. I thought to myself, "They know I'm the secret witness, and they are here to hurt me!"

Jack asked, "Can we come in?" All of a sudden, Tootie came to my side and began to growl. She had never done that before.

"We're not here to cause problems," Jack said.

About that time, my mom pulled up, walked up on the porch and said, "Come on in boys!" What would they do, or think, if they knew I was the only witness against them!

Jack said, "We are here to say, thank you. We found out that you are the donor."

Years of ugly, hateful things I wanted to say to him no longer seemed important. I almost felt sorry for them, knowing that if my bone marrow saved Jack, my testimony would not save him from another injustice.

Jim was to the point of tears when he said, "We don't deserve your kindness." Then he covered his face and wept.

My mom stood up and walked over to him, put her arms around him and said, "It's going to be all right."

"All the mean things we did and said to you throughout your life were unacceptable. I'm ashamed to say that we haven't gotten any better, and sometimes I think we are worse." Jim said, barely able to get the words out.

I thought to myself, "If confession is good for the soul, Jim may tell everything before this night is over."

Jack stood up and said, "Let's go."

When they left, Mom closed the door, walked past me on the way to the kitchen and whispered, "God never ceases to amaze!"

I went to my room and prepared to go to bed. I kissed Tootie and said my prayer, "Oh God, watch over Jack and I during the surgery. We are both in your hands, and for me, there's no better place to be. Amen."

The next day, I had to check in the hospital by two o'clock. I was trying to prepare myself mentally for my decision. It was almost one o'clock when I told my mom we needed to go!

She yelled back, "I'm putting a few things in your bag. I'm almost through."

While we were on our way, she tried to tell me what a good thing I was doing, and that she was very proud that I chose to help Jack.

I could tell that she was worried. She was talking non-stop and wiping her eyes at the same time. When all my paper work was done, I told her to go home, and I would see her in the morning.

She hugged my neck, kissed my cheek and said, "I love you, and I'm more proud than I've ever been in my life. Your father would be, too!"

The attendant came with a wheel chair and Mom left. I was told that I had a semi-private room and another man was already there. When we got to the room, the curtain between us was drawn, and I couldn't see him.

I put on my gown, climbed in bed and turned on the television. I was just lying there when someone knocked on the door. It was Joey. "Come in and sit a while," I told him.

We talked for a minute then he said, "I came here to ask you one question. Why would you save him after all the terrible things he did to us?"

"At first, I didn't want to be tested, but I believe everyone deserves a chance to live," I replied to his question.

Joey's face turned red as he said, "He was always mean to everybody, but especially to us. He beat me up one time and took my money on top of everything else that he did to me. I've hated him for years!"

"Enough of that!" I told him. "He can't hurt us anymore. He's fighting for his life!"

About that time, Brother Paul came in with a smile and said, "Looks like you guys are trying to solve the problems of the world."

We both laughed, and Joey turned to walk out. Brother Paul said, "Let's all pray before you leave. All of us, Jack, too!"

He pulled the curtain back and there was Jack! I almost fell out. I had no idea he was my roommate. Brother Paul said, "Bow your heads please." Then he began.

"There's no limit to God's mercy. A life of hate has no comparison to a life of joy. We must all find a way to forgive even though forgetting will take time. No one in this room is here by mistake. This moment was written by God, before any of you were born. It's up to all of you to write the ending of this story. Amen."

The room got very quiet. Then Jack got out of bed, walked over to Joey and held out his hand and asked, "Please forgive me, for all the terrible things I did to you. I have no excuse other than being a fool."

Joey shook his hand and with tears in his eyes replied, "I'll try." He looked at me and said, "Good luck tomorrow." Then he walked out of the room.

Jack shook Brother Paul's hand and commented, "It's as if I'm trying to right all my wrongs before I die."

I looked at Jack and said, "Oh no, big boy. You're not getting off that easy. You owe me big time when this is all over. I might even give you some of my blind genes!"

We all had a good laugh. Then Jack and I shook hands. Brother Paul looked up as he turned to walk out of the room and whispered, "God never ceases to amaze me!"

Jack walked back to his bed and pulled the curtain closed between us. Before long our room was full of friends and family wishing us well tomorrow.

Jack's family stopped at my bed and thanked me for helping save Jack's life. Little did they know that within a few weeks, I could be the one to change his life again!

Anna sat on my side of the bed, and Mom sat on the other side. Anna made my heart race and no doubt that I would have sweet dreams of her tonight!

When visiting hours were over, I turned on the television and turned the volume down low. The Colts were playing the Giants. Brother against brother, this was going to be a great game.

I was pulling for the Giants because their quarterback came from my favorite college! Ole Miss! The score was tied with ten minutes to go in the fourth quarter.

The quarterback drew back and threw a thirty yard pass, and the receiver caught it as he ran out of bounds. All of a sudden, the referee threw a flag and said, "Incomplete, he was out of bounds!"

I yelled out, "Are you crazy! He was in bounds when he caught that ball!"

Instantly, Jack pulled the curtain back. I couldn't take my eyes off of him. He jumped up from his bed, ran over to me, and when we were nose to nose he grabbed my arm and said, "You can see can't you? When did this happen?"

Without thinking, I looked him in the eyes and said, "A few weeks before you threw me in the back of that van and took your mask off!"

He stood there as if he was frozen in time. Then he put his head down, went back to his bed and pulled the curtain closed. When the game was over, Jack pulled the curtain back and sat on his bed facing me.

He asked, "Why save me if you are going to help send me to prison?"

I shook my head and responded, "You put me in a prison of your meanness most of my life, and now you want my sympathy! You should be thankful that you may only have to face one death sentence!"

He stood up, drew his fist back and walked toward me. Then he stopped. As he turned back toward his bed, he fell to his knees and wept.

I got out of bed, walked over to him and put my hand on his shoulder and whispered, "I'm going to help you in more ways than one, if I can."

Barely able to catch his breath, he pulled himself up off the floor and lay across the bed. I looked at him and said, "Let's end this right now! I have been given a miracle of my sight, and you've been given one, too!"

About that time, Brother Paul and Russell Allen came in the room. Brother Paul sensed the tension and asked, "What's going on in here guys?"

Russell Allen looked at Jack and said, "We think you and Jim were involved in the bank robbery and the marihuana field. As soon as you recover from surgery, we need to talk, and you should have a lawyer present."

"Why save my life? If the only way I can live it is in prison?" Jack asked. "If confession is good for the soul, then let me fight for my life tomorrow with a clear conscience!" He began to tell a story that shocked us all!

"A year ago, I found out that I had cancer. I felt that it was God's revenge for all the terrible things I had done. I knew that fighting this cancer would be a huge financial burden on my family.

"My dad always told me that the money in his bank was insured, and if he was robbed the money would be replaced. One of my customers at the car lot offered me a chance to invest in his marihuana business. I would provide the vehicles for transporting the pot and he would sell it. It was stored in one of my buildings and moved out when it was sold.

"I did these things out of stupidity and fear. What would happen to my family if I died from this cancer? How would they live? I'll be ruined when all this comes out. My father will be, too.

"There's no excuse for what I did to Bud. People showed him more love and compassion than they ever showed me. I was jealous and a fool!

"I hid the money from the bank robbery and the money from the sale of the marihuana. All this is on me. Don't blame my family."

Russell Allen said, "That's enough. You both need to rest. We'll talk when you've both recovered."

As they were leaving the room, Brother Paul turned to both of us and said, "I'm looking at two blessed men. When God shows up, He shows out!"

When Brother Paul closed the door, Jack pulled the curtain and not another word was said.

The sound of people coming in and out woke me. I looked at the clock on the wall and it was five thirty. They were there to get us ready for surgery. As they pulled Jack's bed out, he asked them to stop.

With tears on his cheeks barely able to speak, he softly said, "Forgive me and thank you."

I got out of bed and stood beside him and replied, "I forgive you. You owe me dinner when all this is over." As if it was planned we both gave each other a thumbs up, knowing we were in God's hands now.

Years of hatred were over. Not forgotten, but forgiven. Jack's family and my mom and Anna were standing by the doors leading into the surgery area. Our beds were almost side by side as we spoke to our families.

When the doors opened, Jack and I looked at each other and did a high five! I can't imagine what they thought about that!

When I woke up in the recovery room, Mom and Anna were standing beside the bed. Mom said, "Everything went fine, for you and Jack. He's in intensive care for a few days."

Anna kissed my hand and said, "They're taking you to a room in thirty minutes. We'll see you there." I was lying there thanking God that we both survived the surgery when a shadow covered my face.

I looked up and there was Jack's father. He just stood there for a minute and then he said, "You had every right to want revenge, but you chose to help Jack. You are the type of man I always wanted him to be." Then he wept as he walked away.

The next time I woke up. I was in my room. Mom, Anna and Brother Paul were there. I told Mom and Anna to go get them something to eat because I needed to talk to Brother Paul.

I told Brother Paul that my heart was breaking for Jack and his family. If everything came out, and he was sent to prison, what would his wife and daughter do? I knew that he was scared, but we knew why he did what he did, even though it wasn't right.

Mom and Anna came back and stayed until visiting hours were over. As they were leaving, the doctor came in and told me I could go home tomorrow.

Anna smiled and said, "I'll pick you up tomorrow! Sleep well!"

I was feeling pretty good, so I decided to get up and take a walk. I really wanted some updates on Jack. I called for a nurse to help me because for a few more days everyone needed to still believe that I was blind.

Doing the right thing paid off because I got a pretty nurse, and she smelled good, too! She told me that Jack was stable and his family was with him.

Chapter Twenty-Three

The doctor came in and gave me my discharge papers and told me to come see him for a check in two weeks. There was a knock on the door and thinking it was Anna I said, "Come on in sweetheart!"

Joey stuck his head in the door, laughed and said, "Better be careful, people will talk." I told him I was going home, and Anna was coming to pick me up.

"I'll go, and see you at home sometime." Joey replied.

"Visit with me till Anna gets here and we'll all walk out together." I told him. A few minutes later, Anna came through the door with a wheelchair. She said, "Your ride is here. Let's go!"

I looked up at her and replied, "That chair is not necessary." Then Joey laughed and said, "Get in and I'll drive!"

On our way to the elevator, we passed Jack's family in the hallway. A little girl turned, and began to walk toward me. She had long blonde hair and a beautiful face. As she got closer, the lights in the ceiling reflected off the metal braces on both her legs. Joey stood there and never took his eyes off of her!

When she got to me, she put her hand on mine and said, "My name is Penny. Thank you, for helping my dad. I can't wait for him to come home! I love him."

Tears filled my eyes as I replied, "You're welcome." Then she hugged my neck, and as she let go, she touched my face wiping away a tear, then with a big smile she whispered, "Don't be sad, today's a happy day!"

At that moment I remembered how I felt when I lost my dad. I knew that Jack had a chance to recover, and I prayed he did if for no one else but her.

When we all got in the elevator, Joey began to cry like a baby. Anna put her arm around him and asked, "What's wrong?"

Joey was trying to compose himself and finally managed to say, "My God, My God, she reminds me of myself!"

Anna looked at Joey and said, "Penny was born with multiple sclerosis. She will wear those braces for the rest of her life and her condition could get worse."

When we got to the lobby, Joey walked out and never said another word, not even good-bye. Looking at Jack's little girl really hit Joey hard. When Anna got me home it was getting dark. She hugged me and said, "Get your rest and we'll talk tomorrow."

I went to bed and tried to sleep, but I found myself staring out my window. It was raining and the sky was filled with an incredible lightning show. I wondered about justice and what it really meant.

I wondered if Jack had payed enough for all the mean things he had done. I was given a second chance and maybe he should be, too. Did he deserve one? I guess that's God's call to make.

I needed to talk to Russell Allen and Brother Paul. For some reason, I felt compelled to help him. There was no doubt that Penny made me stop and think about a lot of things. God bless her.

After breakfast the next morning, I asked my mom to take me to Calvary because I needed to talk to Brother Paul. "Is everything ok?" she asked.

I replied, "God is working on my heart, and I'm confused."

When we got to Calvary, Mom said, 'I'll be back shortly, I need to run some errands." She opened my car door, took my arm and handed me my cane and said, "Remember, you are still blind to everyone but a few of us!"

When I walked in the lobby, Brother Paul was waiting. "Come on and we'll talk in my office." He said.

I shook my head no and replied, "Let's do this in the sanctuary. I don't want us to be disturbed." We sat on the front row and Brother Paul patiently waited for me to begin.

I looked him straight in the eyes and asked, "What should I do? I know enough to send Jack to prison for a long time, but revenge is no longer in my heart. There has to be a way to help him."

Brother Paul replied, "I must answer your question with a question! What would Jesus do?"

"He has a wife, daughter and family. I know the truth, and I wish I didn't. Suppose there was a way to make all of this right, and Jack and Jim didn't have to go to prison?" I said.

"Anything is possible with God. You can't blame yourself for telling the truth. Everything good is in God's time, not ours. Tomorrow is never promised. All we have is today," Brother Paul replied.

About that time, Mom walked in the sanctuary and I whispered to Brother Paul, "Please talk to Russell Allen. I know you'll talk to God!"

When we got home, Russell Allen was sitting on the porch. I thought, "Fast work, Brother Paul!" Mom let Tootie out then went inside and made us each a glass of iced tea.

"Suppose," I asked, "there was a way to make things right, and neither Jack nor Jim would have to go to prison? We know that Jack did these things out of desperation for his family, and in the event he died.

"It doesn't make it right, but most people will understand. If they took the money back to the bank and turned state's evidence against the drug dealers, wouldn't their punishment be less?

Russell Allen said, "It's a long shot. How do we know they will be willing to admit to everything, regardless of their consequences? A good attorney would never let them confess without a deal. The F.B.I. would have to agree."

I asked, "Please, please, can you get together with them and ask?" Russell Allen smiled at me and replied, "You surprise me!"

A few days later, I needed to get out of the house for a while, so Anna came by, and we took a drive. I said, "This may sound strange, but I want to go to my father's grave, if that's ok with you."

When we got there, I took it all in as we walked. There were huge shade trees blocking the warm sunshine and beautiful flowers on the graves. For the first time, I was seeing my father's grave.

My eyes filled with tears, and words from deep within my soul spilled out. Memories drove me to my knees, and I seemed to lose my breath. I listened for his voice, but I didn't hear it. I took my hand and traced the letters of his name.

Anna walked away as if to give me some private time. It seemed as if she knew what I needed before I did. I closed my eyes and thought of the memories that made him so much more than a name.

Every time we came here, Mom always said, "Don't be sad. God is watching over him." But she cried. I realized how selfish I had been. I never thought about the depth of her loss and how sad she's been all these years.

I heard someone calling my name, it was Anna. She asked, "Are you ready to go? It will soon be dark." As we walked back to her car. I put my arms around her and asked, "What did I do to deserve you?"

Mom was waiting on the porch when we got back. Tootie jumped off the porch and came running up to me. She did her usual and jumped up on me, wanting some love. I am so blessed.

Mom told me that she heard that Jack was going home tomorrow and was doing very well! I couldn't help but think that within a few days, the truth would come out. My deception, too!

Russell Allen called the next morning and asked me to come to the courthouse. He was waiting for me when I got there. He took me to a conference room full of people. They were with the F.B.I. and D.E.A.

Before the questions started, Russell Allen said, "Take your time, answer truthfully only what you are positive about. If you aren't sure about something, make sure you say that. Answer their questions, but don't elaborate!"

He clasped my hand and asked, "You do understand what I'm telling you and why I'm saying this?"

I smiled at him and said, "I got it!"

They asked so many questions I couldn't answer, but the ones I did answer made me nervous. Before they excused me from the room, they told me not to speak of our conversation here today.

One of the men commented that having two witnesses would be a good thing. He patted me on the shoulder and said, "In most cases one of the brothers will turn on the other."

Russell Allen and I walked out of the room and he whispered, "They have enough to prosecute them and I expect that within a week or so, they will be served subpoenas to appear before the Grand Jury."

As I turned to walk away, I saw Joey going in the court house. I thought, "Walk over and see if he can do lunch!" When I got to the area he worked in, there was total chaos!

He looked up and saw me standing there and said, "It's a mad house in here and it's getting worse!"

I told him, "Call my mom and asked her not to pick me up for a while, and let's you and I do lunch!"

A few minutes later, we walked over to the café and got a table. I asked him, "What's going on in your area? People are everywhere!"

Joey shook his head and said, "They are transferring all paper documents to C.D.'s, shredding old paper work and moving files to another part of the court house. I don't think the left hand knows what the right hand is doing! This is the biggest mess I've ever seen!"

We ordered our lunch, and Joey told me that he couldn't get Penny off his mind. He knew what she was facing from cruel people, and it brought back memories of how he was treated by some people.

Joey said, "I'm trying to find a way to forgive him if only for Penny, but it's hard. I know what is coming down for both of them because I've seen the documents!"

"Don't you think everyone deserves a second chance?" I asked him.

He looked at me and replied, "Yes, everyone deserves God's mercy!"

About that time, Jack and Jim walked in the café. They saw us and walked toward our table. Joey and I looked at each other but didn't say a word.

Jack's lips began to tremble as he spoke, "In a matter of days, my life will change forever because of some things I've done. I have a favor to ask of both of you. If you see anyone being cruel to Penny like I was to the both of you, please help her!" He wept as they walked away from the table.

We just sat there! "Back to work!" Joey said. I picked up our ticket and replied, "I got this one. Have a good day. Call my mom and tell her to and get me."

My head hurt, I was sick to my stomach and I wanted to scream. When the news got out about all of this, the place we called home, and the people we called friends, were going to change.

Things were pretty quiet for the next few days. I could read almost anything and tell you all the colors. Mom was a genius!

Anna and I spent almost every evening and weekend together. I was falling in love with her, and I knew she felt the same way. I would have never imagined being able to see, or falling in love.

I'll never forget it was a Wednesday morning while Mom and I were having coffee at the kitchen table when Russell Allen came to the house. I knew in my heart that something was about to happen.

He told me that on Friday I had to appear before the Grand Jury to testify. It was all coming down in two days. He would pick me up and bring me home when it was all over.

When he left, Mom said, "This is out of your control. Just tell the truth and it will work out. You're not to blame for their actions. The best thing you can do is pray."

I got up the next morning nauseated. For a moment, just a moment, I wish I had been blind that day. "Two days," I thought. "I could ruin the life I just helped save."

Mom put her arms around me and said, "You can't change what Jack and Jim did, but you can pray for God's mercy on both of them."

Chapter Twenty-Four

Friday morning, Russell Allen came and picked me up. It was a quiet ride to the courthouse. He knew I was nervous. When we walked in, everyone involved in the case was there.

Jack and Jim sat at the table with their attorney. Their family was in the first row behind them.

I sat on the opposite side behind the prosecutor's table. No one else was visible in the court room. Where were Russell Allen, the District Attorney and the F.B.I.?

I couldn't help looking at Jack and Jim's families, knowing that my testimony was going to send them to prison.

As if it wasn't bad enough, Penny came over to me and hugged my neck. Then she asked in a whisper with her hand clasped around my ear, "Are you going to help my daddy again?"

I wanted to cry. I looked her in the eyes, smiled as I replied, "I hope your daddy is going to be just fine!" She walked away, and I looked at my watch. We had been there an hour. Where was everyone else?

All of a sudden, the door to the Judge's chambers opened. Russell Allen and the men with the F.B.I. came in the courtroom. When everyone was seated, the judge asked Russell Allen to be sworn and take the witness stand.

The prosecutor and defense attorney both stood to address the court. The judge said, "Be seated, you'll understand in a minute."

The judge addressed Russell Allen and asked for an update on the circumstances of this case.

Russell Allen began, "Some very strange things have happened in the last forty eight hours. The money that was stolen from the bank was returned in the middle of the night. It was in a box with two black water pistols in the bottom.

"The surveillance tapes from the drive through and the bank are missing, and last night the marihuana field and cabin were burnt to the ground! We don't have enough evidence to prosecute the defendants at this time."

The judge looked at the prosecutor and asked, "Can you explain to me how all your evidence disappeared?"

He stood and replied, "That document room is in chaos! We're adding on the new part of the building for storage. There are twelve part-time people helping transfer documents to C.D.'s and then they shred the old ones. Boxes are everywhere and there is no telling what has been misplaced, or destroyed!"

I was sitting there holding my breath! I just shook my head and thought, "Unbelievable!"

The judge said, "Your people were in charge of this evidence! No evidence! No case! Dismissed!"

I got up and walked out of the courtroom, and Brother Paul was waiting. He asked, "Is it over?" With a smile on my face I replied, "It never began!"

We sat down, and I told him everything that happened. He just turned his head from side to side, then I commented, "Don't you find it strange that everything disappeared hours before this hearing, and only a few people knew about it!"

"No doubt there was an angel working overtime in this case!" Brother Paul said as we left the courthouse. I said a few hallelujahs myself! Brother Paul took me home, where Mom and Anna were waiting for some news.

I told them what happened, and they both cried. Mom hugged my neck and said, "It's over now. We can all move on."

Anna chimed in and replied, "Jack and Jim are two lucky men. We'll see if this changes their attitudes!"

Brother Paul said, "Hallelujah" as he got in his truck and left.

I felt such a relief that this was all over. My secret had to come out now, and I was glad. I wanted to get on with my life, hopefully, a life with Anna.

Sunday morning was a great time of celebration at Calvary Church. At the end of the service, Brother Paul called for Jack and me to come down front. He stood between us and said, "You are looking at two of God's miracles. Jack's bone marrow transplant has been successful, and Bud's sight is coming back in bits and pieces!"

There was an uproar in the sanctuary! "Praise God" and "Amen" overpowered Brother Paul's voice while God's people gave Him praise!

Jack shook my hand as his chin quivered and he managed to say, "Thank you for saving my life." I hugged him and whispered, "God gave us both a miracle. Good luck."

The congregation stood and clapped as we walked back to our seats. When I got to where Joey was sitting, I stopped. I held out my hand to shake his and said, "Forgiveness is a wonderful thing. The burden of hatred is gone from my heart."

Joey smiled as he wiped a tear from his face and replied, "Mine, too!"

If I learned anything through all of this it was that anger holds you back from being the best that you can be. I wanted to live now and pursue a life with Anna.

I put my cane and dark glasses away. Tootie retired and became just my dog. I hoped and prayed that I could keep my sight. The world and people I looked at around me were amazing!

Anna and I became inseparable. Christmas was just around the corner, and I needed to find her the perfect gift. I told Mom that I loved Anna and wanted to marry her. She replied, "This is not news to me!"

She took my hand and said, "I want to help you. I saved all the money from your father's settlement. You can buy her a beautiful ring and a house. There's more than enough!"

I never imagined that my mom would offer us such a gift. I hugged her neck and cried. She said, "This money has always been for you. Let's do it up right. Your father would approve."

Christmas Eve, Anna came over and helped us decorate the Christmas tree. I was in awe of its beauty. I had never seen one before! Mom described every ornament ever given me, and the ones she helped me make as a blind child.

After we all had a cup of hot chocolate, Mom excused herself and gave Anna and I some time alone. I held her in my arms and told her how much I loved her.

She cried and told me that she loved me, too! I walked over to the tree, picked up a present and said, "This is for you. Open it!"

When she opened the box, a smaller one was inside. She went through two more boxes and found a note. It read, "Turn and look at me!"

When she turned and looked at me, I was on one knee holding open a ring box with a beautiful diamond ring. I held it up and said, "This could be yours, but you have to say, "You'll marry me!"

She must have said, "Oh my God," twenty times and then she screamed, "Yes!" so loud that Mom came back in the room and replied, "Finally!" We all hugged each other and Mom left the room saying, "See y'all in the morning!"

It was after midnight when Anna left. Her family was coming here for Christmas dinner tomorrow. I took Tootie outside and we looked at the stars in the sky. Tears filled my eyes as I whispered, "Dad, oh how I wish you were here, but I know you are watching. I love you and miss you. Though you will not be at my side the day of our wedding, you'll always be my best man."

Christmas dinner was the best! Our families were excited about the wedding. Both our moms were already planning the whole thing! Anna and I laughed and thought, "Let them do the work and enjoy themselves. There's no doubt that it will turn out perfect!"

Mom shocked us all when she offered to pay for everything! "If Bud and Anna agree, it would be my pleasure to do this in Kirby's name. Let's make this a wedding they will never forget!" Then we all cried.

Anna and I looked around and found a two bedroom house to rent until we could find one to buy. Mom, Anna and Mary Helen had it fixed up in no time. Everything was going good. I prayed it stayed that way.

The next few months both our moms were having the time of their life. They took Anna to pick out her dress and everything else. They told us that we needed to pick the people for our wedding party.

Chapter Twenty-Five

Every Sunday morning at church, Jack and Jim would stop at our pew, say good morning and shake my hand. More surprisingly then, they would walk down front, speak to Joey and shake his hand! Maybe God's mercy had changed their hearts.

Penny would hug my neck and say, "Have a happy day!" then she would do the same to Anna and Mom.

Later that afternoon, Anna and I talked about who we wanted in our wedding party. I told her that I had two suggestions and wanted her opinion. "I would love to ask Joey to be my best man and Penny to be our flower girl."

Anna threw her arms around my neck, kissed my face and replied, "Great idea, I love it!" I told her that I would talk to Joey, and we should talk to Jack.

The next morning, I went to the courthouse to talk to Joey. I went to the document room, and he was standing by the copier. He looked up and I asked, "Can I talk to you for a minute?"

"Sure," he said. Then we walked over to a table and sat down. "I need a favor," I told him. "I need a best man to stand up for me at my wedding, and you're the best man I know!"

He covered his face to hide his emotion and then with tears in his eyes he replied, "No one has ever asked me to be a part of anything. I would be honored."

I stood up, shook his hand and said, "We'll talk soon and thank you. You've made my day!" I left hoping that I had made his day, too!

After supper, Anna and I drove to Jack's house. They invited us in and when Penny saw me she did her usual and gave me a big hug. Anna looked at Jack and said, "We need a very special favor! We need a flower girl for our wedding, and we would love for it to be Penny!"

Jack was speechless for a moment, then he replied, "We would be honored. Let's ask Penny."

I called her over to me, sat her on my lap and asked, "Anna and I are getting married, and we need a beautiful flower girl. Will you be our flower girl?"

She hugged me so tight that she almost choked me then she said, "I'll need a new dress, new shoes, flowers to carry and yes, yes, yes!" Everybody in the room had tears in their eyes. Penny looked around and yelled out, "No tears! It's going to be a happy day!"

When Anna and I got up to leave, Jack wiped the tears from his face, shook my hand and whispered, "I am in awe of the kindness you've shown Penny. I am so sorry I never showed that to you."

"Water under the bridge," I said. "That was then, this is now!"

Anna took Penny by the hand and said, "I will come and get you in a week. We'll go pick your dress, shoes, flowers and a beautiful bow for your hair!" Then we said our good-byes and left.

I laughed as I put my arms around Anna and said, "We got that piece done. Now we need to go talk to Brother Paul and after that we say, I do!" She threw her arms up in the air and replied, "Amen, too, I do!"

We decided to get married on Valentine;s Day. It was going to be at Calvary Church. Both our parents were married there and we would be too!

I'll never forget the day we went and talked to Brother Paul. He told us about both our parents wedding ceremonies and especially, their vows! He laughed as he told us. We could just imagine what he had in store for us!

Three weeks before the wedding, both our moms got together and gave us a wedding shower. We got so many gifts that we put them in the spare bedroom of our house and almost filled it up. We decided to wait until we got back from our honeymoon to open them.

The rehearsal dinner was crazy! It just happened to fall on the night that Ole Miss and LSU played each other! If you could only imagine Brother Paul in purple pants, a purple shirt, a gold tie and purple socks!

Mine wasn't much better! A red tie, blue shirt, red pants and blue socks! Anna laughed and said, "Are you guys celebrating the game, or this wedding?" Neither one of us responded. We both just smiled! Just being a part of this wedding party was worth this!

The next morning was a rush for me. At eleven o'clock we were getting married. We decided to have an early wedding because Mom was giving us a special honeymoon trip, and we had to be at the airport by five o'clock.

I don't even want to know what my mom spent on our wedding, but it was magical. Anna's dress was breath taking, and Penny looked like a little princess. As usual the flowers were like a beautiful picture of a garden. Ms. Ava Sue had really outdone herself. Ms. Patricia catered the food, and it was so good that people ate more than they talked!

The highlight of the wedding was when Brother Paul said, "You may kiss your bride!" He started laughing. Then he raised his pants leg up and there were those purple socks!

Everyone in the sanctuary stood and clapped! Once again he stole the show, and his team won the ball game, too! At least I was the winner today!

Anna's father made the toast to us and it was unforgettable. "To Bud and Anna. I could've never imagined that this type of love would show itself for a third time." He raised his glass toward the ceiling and said with great emotion, "I know you're watching, Kirby, and you are smiling down on Bud and Anna. I will love them and watch over them as long as I live!"

We both hugged him and cried. It was getting time for us to go, so Anna threw the bouquet, and we left to change clothes. As we were walking down the steps leaving the church a limo was waiting. I thought, "Way to go, Mom." I put my arms around her, and she wept. She kissed my face and said, "Aloha!"

I picked Anna up in my arms, swung her around and yelled, "We're going to Hawaii. A week in heaven on earth!" We held each other all the way to the airport planning what we were going to do and anxiously awaiting the first time we made love.

Every dream we had ever had, came true in those seven days. I only thought I knew what love was. I wasn't prepared for the bliss that God gives to a husband and wife.

When Anna and I got back from our honeymoon. She said, "I'll start dinner and you can bring all the gifts in the kitchen, and we'll open them. Be sure and bring a tablet and piece of paper to write the names down, so we can send thank you cards."

Before I could respond there was a knock on the door. It was our parents. "Come on in you're just in time because Anna needs some help!" Mom and Mary Helen helped Anna while J.D. and I went and sat on the porch.

When J.D. and I walked back inside, they were cleaning up all the wrapping paper. There was one gift left on the table. I hugged Anna and said, "Let me help you baby!" We all had a good laugh then our parents left.

Anna said, "I'm really tired so I'm going to take a bath since you've got this under control."

The gift wasn't wrapped very well and there was no card on it. I thought it was a gag gift, or a booby trap for me! I was almost sure that when I opened it something would pop out, or get my finger!

I took all the wrapping off and the box was taped. I thought, "This is interesting!" I got a knife and cut the tape. All I could see was shredded paper. I pulled out a hand full very carefully and put it on the table.

I continued to pull out the contents a handful at a time. After a minute I took a close look at this paper and there was something else shredded in there too! Its texture changed. It was like film pieces and pictures, not just paper!

All of a sudden, my heart began to race. I sat down and took a deep breath! I asked myself, "Could this be what I think it is?" I continued to empty the box a handful at a time.

I had almost all of it out when I saw a folded piece of paper in the bottom. I pulled out the piece of paper, took a deep breath and opened it!

Tears filled my eyes as I read the words written on it. "And now, I see!"

Bio

Born and raised in Mississippi, Margaret Eubanks still resides there today with her adopted dog, Tootie.

She is the author of eight books, available in paperback and on Kindle –

Whispers

Good Night, Sippi, I Love You

Ankepi: The Keeper of the Angel Wall

Ankepi II: All is Revealed

The Tattered Bag: A Life Remembered

The Never Ending Road

The Never Ending Road II: A Promise is Kept and a Gift is Delivered

And Now I See

Made in the USA
Lexington, KY
28 August 2017